SENSELESS ATTRACTION

USA TODAY BESTSELLING AUTHOR
LILA ROSE

Editing: Hot Tree Editing
Formatting: Lee Ching with Under Cover Designs
ISBN: 978-0-6484960-6-9

Justine Littleton
Without you Senseless Attraction would not have made sense!
Thank YOU!!!
You are a wonderful, sarcastic person and my life would be a lot duller without you in it. You know I love you!

PART ONE

ONE

SKYLAR

I really wanted to stay home. I already knew there'd be no good with attending, but why delay the inevitable? No matter what day I went, I'd still have to find out who my new history partner would be. Still, just the thought of it made my stomach churn. Because everyone knew, Mr Gavin was known for pairing up the wrong type of people for the midterm assignment. So no doubt, I'd end up with someone who was the total opposite to me. Someone snotty, over-classed, popular, and who wouldn't be caught dead speaking to the likes of me.

I lived in a small, three-bedroom brick home with my momma. It was nothing to rave about, but it kept us warm at night, and really, I couldn't help but love the place. Momma and I had made it our own. We moved in a year ago when my father ran off with his secretary, leaving us high and dry.

Momma had to take on a job; she worked night shifts at our local supermarket, stocking shelves and sometimes at the register. At least it was something she loved doing. And being night work, it was enough money to keep the banks off our heels.

"Skylar James, hurry up with that God-awful makeup and get your butt in here for breakfast," Momma bellowed from the kitchen. She didn't need to yell; my bedroom was only a door away. I could even hear a normal conversation going on, like the ones where Momma would sit there with her friends and complain about my dad. She'd never figured out I could hear. It killed me when I heard her crying sometimes.

I walked out of my room and straight into the kitchen to find her at the stove still wearing her work uniform. She had only walked in the door an hour earlier.

She turned and sighed. "Tell me again why you wear that stuff? It clogs up all your pores, and you're too beautiful for it anyway."

I rolled my eyes as she placed a plateful of eggs and bacon in front of me on the table.

Yeah. I snorted. *Me, beautiful? I don't think so.* My hair was too black and too straight. My body was too fatty and too tall. I had no boobs to gloat about, and way too much ass. The only thing I liked about myself was my dark, leafy-green eyes.

"Momma, you know why. One, I like it, and two, it makes the other kids at school stay away from me. They think I'm a witch or something."

She scoffed. "I may start thinking that myself. Should I be checking your room for voodoo dolls?"

Again, I rolled my eyes as she laughed at her own joke. She knew she could trust me not to fall into any of that sort of stuff.

The makeup she was referring to was the white powdered foundation I used on my face. It also helped me hide the deep two-centimetre-long scar I had on my forehead that I got when I was six after a skateboard accident. My long, in-the-eyes, black fringe assisted to cover it as well. Wearing black eyeliner and black lipstick was just a preference of mine. It matched the style in which I liked to dress. Like today, I had chosen ankle boots with black fishnet tights, a short tartan skirt, and a black t-shirt. It was still summer, so I wouldn't need my long black jacket.

"Hurry up and eat, girl, or you'll be late for the bus." Momma gave me a quick kiss on the cheek. "I'm going for a shower, and I'll see you tonight. Have a good day, hon," she called over her shoulder as she headed down the hall to the bathroom.

"Yeah right," I muttered.

I finished my plate, rinsed it, and quickly raced out the door as the bus travelled up my street. Right out the front of my house was the last stop before Freddy, the Santa- looking bus driver, dropped us off at school. His route took him to the snob zone first because they lived on the west side – the farther side – where all the mansions and estates were. I lived on a normal street that contained the smaller houses that were close to one another.

Climbing onto the bus that would take me to my wonderful school—*feel the sarcasm?*—Mt. Henry, I showed my bus pass, and gave a small chin lift to Freddy. He grunted back, and then I sat down in the first seat up at the front, next to my friend Jessie Mitanni. I didn't bother looking in the back anymore, knowing that if I did, all I would receive is laughs and glares. Besides, the one I used to look for no longer attended our school. Actually, he no longer lived on the same continent.

A high-pitched squeal touched my ears, causing me to shudder. I knew straight away who it was, Miss Donna Evans, the most popular girl in school. And I knew who she'd be sitting with, Kane Stanley, her rich—well, richer than her by a little—boyfriend, and some of their evil posse who chose to ride the bus with them.

"S'up?" Jessie asked while applying her black lipstick. Unlike my momma, her mom couldn't stand her wearing any of this sort of makeup, so Jessie applied it in the mornings and removed it before heading home. At least her mom wasn't so grouchy when it came to the clothes both Jessie and I wore.

I found that it suited Jessie more, with her slim figure, medium height, dark blonde hair, and light blue eyes. She was even lucky enough to have been visited by the boob fairy.

"Not much, you?" I asked as I skidded down lower in my seat.

"Usual. God, I hate Mondays."

"Tell me about it. I wish I caught some very long-lasting disease over the weekend, and then I wouldn't have to deal with being matched up with a partner in history today."

"Oh, man, that's today? I feel for ya; I have that Friday."

"Just pray for me that I don't get any of those asses in the back." I gestured with my head towards the back of the bus.

"I'll pray as long as you do it for me. At least you know there's no chance of getting Trevor, Beth, or Megan, 'cause they're in my class."

"Yeah, but they're the better out of the lot."

"True, too true." She nodded. "You have it first period, yeah?"

"Yep." I sighed loudly.

"Best wishes, Sky. See ya at lunch." She gave me a wink and flew past me to get off the bus. I just wasn't in the mood to move. I waited until the last person had stomped off, and then dragged my reluctant form from the bus to—*da-da-daaa*—History.

I walked straight to my table in the middle of the class that I shared with another friend of mine, Mitch. Even though we were in the same classes most of the time, he should have actually been in year twelve. He was asked to repeat a year, so that made him eighteen, where I was still—*cry*—seventeen. Mitch and I got along really well. He had even chosen to hang with Jessie and me instead of the other crowd in year twelve that he used to hang with. Well, except for Javis, a skate-boarder friend, and Massie, a girl who was into the same things as Jessie and me. Another reason Mitch was hanging around with us was because of a certain crush he had going for Jessie. Not that she was aware of it, or the fact that I'd figured it out, but I did hope he would make a move. They'd be good for each other.

"Wad'up?" Mitch asked as I sat next to him.

"Fretting, you?"

"Nah, it should be all right. As long as we don't get any of the snobs. Jessie here today?"

I gulped back my laugh and nodded at him as our teacher Mr Gavin walked in. He wasn't bad for a teacher, besides the fact he wanted to try and fix everything by having the idea of 'share your midterm experience with someone you don't know'. He should've known it was useless; we mingled with whom we wanted, and that suited us. Though, no matter how many times students complained, or just didn't do the assignment because of being paired with someone they despised, and then, in turn, failed the half-year assignment, Mr Gavin never backed down by changing. He still thought it was the right thing to do.

"All right, class, we all know what today is. So once I call your names, please, one of you change your table to sit with your new partner. This will not only be for this half-year assignment, but for the rest of the year."

Groans erupted all around, myself included.

I closed my eyes, leaned my head down on the desk, and sent out a silent prayer. *Please, no snob.*

He called names out that I didn't care for, but then he came to Mitch's name, and I had to look up and give Mitch a sympathy pat on the shoulder because he had just been paired with Dale, the class clown. It was going to be so hard to work with him. Poor Mitch would probably have to do all the work himself.

"Skylar James—" I stiffened; here it was. "You are paired with Kane Stanley." Mr Gavin moved on to call out the rest of the class, but I had stopped listening. I think I was in shock. How could he do this to me? Anyone but him would've been better.

"Oh, babe. I feel for you," I heard Donna say.

It must have been obvious I wasn't moving, so Kane had decided to come to me and my table since Mitch had already moved to sit with Dale. The chair next to me was pulled out and Kane Stanley sat down.

"Hi," he said.

"Yeah, hi. I'm, um, Skylar," I uttered, looking at him for the first time. He was your usual jock type: tall, broadly built, with short dark brown hair that hung too long in the front, and nice, warm golden eyes.

Nice? Warm? Where did I pull that from?

He turned his chair a little to face me and smirked, flashing his perfect white teeth. "I know who you are."

Of course, he did; how lame did I sound? But really, it was the first time we'd met, wasn't it? I mean, besides the fact that we'd known each other by association for some time.

I couldn't help but look over my shoulder to see who Donna had been paired with. It was Kevin Meit, one of the smartest kids in school. No fair. She was going to breeze through the assignment by making her partner do all the work.

Would Kane make me do that as well? He could certainly think again if he tried it.

"Now, class. Take this time to talk to your new partner about what you think would be a good subject for this assignment. Remember, I have allowed you to cover anything in History." With that, he sat down, and the talking around us started.

Kane cleared his throat. "So, any ideas?"

"Um," I said while flicking through our textbook. I gave up and sighed. "Nope, none. You?"

He smirked again; how could that make my heart race? Goddamn good-looking jock.

"Let's see. We have options of World War One or Two..."

I rolled my eyes. "Boring."

"Okay then, what about a person from our history?"

"Could work, like who?"

He shrugged. "Hitler, Gandhi, Patrick Henry, Einstein, Thomas Jefferson..."

"Or what about women from history? Like Martha Jane Cannary, Harriet Jacobs, Eleanor Roosevelt, and Victoria Woodhull. And that's only to name some, but I'm sure *we* could look into others."

He let out a quiet laugh. "All right, what about we do both? What about Mrs Roosevelt and her husband?"

"Sounds interesting." And easy.

"When do you want to get together and work?" he asked.

I swallowed loudly and coughed it back up when it went down the wrong way.

After clearing my throat, I said, "Why not here, right now, and then every time we have class?" I was not giving Donna any ammunition to start on me. And if Kane and I worked alone somewhere other than class, it was just asking for trouble.

"It's due in a month, Skylar. We..."

"Sky," I uttered.

"Sorry?"

"Only my momma calls me Skylar. So call me Sky, okay?"

"Sure." He smiled. "As I was saying, we only have a month to do a written assignment, and then an oral; both have to sound totally different from one another. There's a lot to cover for both people, and I don't know about you, but I need a good grade for this class."

"I'm not going to slack off if that's what you're worried about. I'm not like that." I glared. "Fine, where and when do you want to do this?"

"Monday nights are good for me, as well as Saturdays—early mornings though. We can alternate; one day I could come to your house, the other, you come to mine?"

I couldn't help but stare at him. I shut my mouth with an audible click when he started looking confused.

"Look, Kane, it's real nice of you to try this 'partner thing'," I made air quotes, "but I cannot see you coming to my house and playing nice. And I really cannot see myself at your house. Come on. Your parents would freak if I walked in the door, and probably worry I'd steal something."

Okay, he looked angry. "Is that how it is then? You obviously already think I'm some rich asshole who's already judged you not worthy of my time; therefore, we cannot get along enough to get this assignment done." He took a deep breath. "Not all people judge a book by its cover, *Skylar.*" I scoffed and looked to Donna. He snorted and added, "I said *not all.*"

I growled in frustration. Fine. If he wanted to play it that way, he could just come and see how the other side lived. But I would not make it easy on him at all.

"Whatever, Kane Stanley. Let's do this. Come to my house tonight. The address…oh, you should already know. The bus pulls right out in front of it every morning."

"Good. I'll see you there later. I have a few things to do after school first."

"Yeah, sure." More like he was worried that if he got off at my spot, people would start talking.

He rolled his eyes as the bell rang. Donna came up beside our desk and leaned over to give him a big, show-off kiss.

Like I didn't already know she owned his ass.

I walked out of the classroom before they started stripping.

Mitch caught up to me at the door and flung his arm around my shoulders. We had the next class together. "I don't know who dibbed out worse here," he sighed.

"Yeah, me either. Give me a couple of days, though, and I'm sure I'll be ripping my hair out from all the talk about the rich life."

Mitch laughed. "Don't worry, pet. I'll be there doing it with you."

"Hey, punk. Get ya hands off me woman."

I laughed as Javis came up beside us. Mitch didn't move his arm though; we both knew Javis was joking. Like he always did.

"So, what's da verdict?"

"I got Dale, and Princess Puff Cake here got Mr Charming himself, Kane Stanley," Mitch explained.

That was my new nickname. Ever since I ate five puff cakes with cream in one afternoon when we visited the bakery, Fat

Papa's. I wouldn't usually eat that much, but that day I had some extra spending money from my birthday and splurged on my all-time-favourite: puff cakes. For some reason, I couldn't stomach them these days, especially after I spent the night throwing them back up.

"Whoa, no way, man. Damn it, if it's like that for you guys, there's no telling who Jessie's gonna get. Glad I've already been through that last year."

"Yeah, and who were you with?" I asked.

Javis pretended to shudder. "Byney Steill, who I thought was the love of my life at the time." He shrugged and added for me, "Sorry, babe. But once I got to know her, found out she didn't have a brain, and was a robot, it was off. All she could talk about was clothes, Brad Pitt, clothes, Brad Pitt, and..."

"Clothes," both Mitch and I answered.

"Right. Anyway, better fly before I'm late and get into trouble once again. See ya's at lunch."

He ran two doors down where he had Science, as Mitch and I walked into Social Studies.

At lunch, Mitch, Javis, and I walked into the loud, already-busy cafeteria. After grabbing some lunch, we headed to our usual table where Jessie and Massie were seated. As I walked over, I noticed Jessie's somewhat eager expression. I rolled my eyes; she must already have known who my history partner was.

"Princess Puff Cake, you seem to have caught not only Mr Charming's attention, but Miss Evil's as well," Mitch casually said.

I glanced out the corner of my eye to the far corner where all the popular kids hung out, and for some reason, as soon as I saw Kane staring at me, my heart jumped and my stomach started with those annoying butterfly feelings. That was until in the same second, I saw Donna sending her deadly glare my way. If looks could kill, I would be dead. I had no idea what for though. It wasn't like she should feel threatened by me; Kane and I had only met today. No sparks flew when it happened.

"Sky? Sky, come on! Tell all. How lucky are you to get Mr Hottie?" Jessie exclaimed while grabbing my hand and dragging me into the seat next to her.

"I wouldn't say he was hot," I said. Maybe good-looking, but not hot.

"I'd have to agree with you there, Sky. He does nothing for me," Massie mumbled around a mouthful of sandwich.

"Me neither," Mitch said. Jessie glared at him.

"So fill me in; what did he say? Does he sound nice? Or is he a richy and thinks he's too good to talk to you? Come on, spill."

"He seems okay. We talked about the assignment, and that's all of it summed up."

"You're kidding, right? The first chance you have him away from the evil one and you talk about the assignment?"

"Jess, there is nothing else I would want to say to him. Now, let's drop the subject and eat; I'm starved."

She harrumphed, but did as I asked.

"So, plans for the weekend?" Massie asked, since she was the first to finish her lunch.

"It's only Monday, girl. How can I think that far ahead?" Javis smirked.

"True, your brain is only capable of one thing at a time." Jessie laughed. "Well, as you know, Sky and I are going to the fair on Saturday..."

"Not without me you ain't," Mitch growled.

"Keep your knickers on, boy. You can come. And you too, if you want," Jessie said to Javis.

"I can't go so early now," I said, and then shut my mouth quickly.

"Why-y-y?" Jessie drawled.

I sighed. "My history partner wants to meet up Monday nights and Saturday mornings to do as much work as we can get done. Because Mr. Big-and-Strong needs a good grade and is worried I won't pull my own weight in this assignment," I said quickly.

"Mr. Big-and-Strong, hey?" she teased.

"Really? That's all you got out of what I just said?" I complained.

"Yeah, and that you'll be spending quiet time alone with him. Oh, oh, oh! You have to let me come. Please say I can come with you."

"No," both Mitch and I said at the same time. Then I added, "For one, we will be doing work while alone together, so we can't have distractions like you panting all over him. And two, come Friday, you'll be busy enough with your own history partner."

She pouted at me. "Yeah, all right."

TWO

SKYLAR

I didn't know what time Mr Big-Shot was turning up, so I went about my usual afternoon activities. Which included: a snack, a nap, and a lap around the house to see if there was anything incriminating lying about. After doing that, I went and hopped on the family computer, logging in with my password so Momma couldn't check my emails and other stuff. Not that she would really find anything interesting. I ended up receiving an email from Jessie. How could she be home and already sent me an email? She had tennis after school.

Hey Chick, is he there yet?

I laughed and typed back:

No! Talk to you tomorrow.

Before I got the chance to sign off, it dinged back with another email from Jessie. What was she doing, sitting on her computer?

No you don't! You email or call me later about EVERY-THING!!!!!! Or else.

I didn't bother replying; instead, I got up from the desk in the lounge and went to my room to flop on the bed. I should have asked what time he was coming around. Too bad, I only thought of it when I was sitting on the bus, and there was no way I was going to the back of the bus to ask him in front of his Barbie doll girlfriend. I even told myself as I was getting off the bus not to look back there. Too bad my head didn't listen; I snuck a quick glance and wished I hadn't...he was looking at me. I turned away and climbed down the steps.

My other homework called to me. I needed to get it out of the way anyway, and I knew it would keep me busy for a couple of hours.

It had, until I heard a car pull into the driveway. My heart started to pound, but as soon as the front door came open and I heard humming, I knew it was just Momma.

"Skylar, hon, you home?" Momma called from the kitchen. Remembering it had been food-shopping day, I walked out to give her a hand to put away the groceries.

"Hi'ya, Momma. Did you sleep well today?"

"I did indeed. How was your day, sweetheart? God, haven't you taken that stuff off your face yet?" She complained. Usually, that would be the first thing I did when getting home, unless I was meeting my friends later.

"Nope. I have someone coming over—" I began, as a knock at the door interrupted me. My stupid heart began pounding again. I quickly stomped to the door and opened it. Kane stood there smiling, with his arms full of books.

"Hi," he said. "Hope I'm not too late for you."

I looked at the clock over my shoulder that hung in the lounge above our television. It was already half-past five.

"Suppose it'll have to do," I muttered. I grabbed some of the books from him because they seemed like a heavy load, and stepped aside to let him in.

"Sorry, I got caught up with something. Look, if it's going to be a hassle, we can just meet Saturday."

I looked over my shoulder to give him a smart-ass smirk; instead, I was caught up ogling him. He did look good wearing dark blue jeans and a lighter-coloured tee. I turned back around and said, "No, we can't have that; you may think I'm not

pulling my weight. Don't worry about it, okay? Let's get something started." We entered the kitchen where Momma had
already started cooking, but she turned once hearing us enter.

"Momma, this is Kane. Kane, this is Mrs James."

"Nice to meet you, Mrs James." Kane smiled and placed his
books on the table so he could hold out his hand.

To my embarrassment, she stood there in shock, gawking
at him.

"Momma," I hissed. She came out of her semi-trance, and
laughed giddily while she took his hand and shook it vigorously.

"All right, Momma, let go of the poor guy."

She blushed and dropped her hand. "Sorry, dear. Uh, Skylar,
what's going on here?"

I rolled my eyes. "He's here to study; he's my assigned
history partner."

"Oh, well, very good. Skylar, don't just stand there; get the
young man a drink."

Again, I rolled my eyes and went to the fridge, pouring Kane
and myself a drink of Coke. I passed it to him, and he sat at the
table under Momma's instructions.

She nudged me in the side as I sat down next to Kane. "Oh,
honey, he is a looker." She smiled.

I groaned. "Yeah, well, Momma, don't get your hopes up on
grandkiddies just yet. Kane here already has a plastic girlfriend,"
I explained.

Kane frowned at me as he picked up his drink.

Momma gasped. "You mean a blow-up doll?"

Kane coughed and spat his drink all over the table. How
could I not laugh?

"No, Momma, one of those Barbie rich-types."

"Oh, oh well." She turned to Kane, who had gotten up to
grab the paper towel on the bench to wipe his face, then the
table. "That's nice for you, dear." Momma grinned. "And Skylar,
you shouldn't put her down while in his company."

At least she didn't say I shouldn't bag her at all. I think Kane caught onto it as well because he smirked.

"So let's get started before my Momma can say anything else."

"Would you like to stay for tea, Kane?"

Too late.

"That would be nice. Thank you, Mrs James."

"Call me Jenny, dear. Skylar, why don't you take Kane into your room and study there at your desk while I run around the kitchen?"

I looked at Kane's surprised expression.

Normal moms didn't say that kind of stuff. Whose Momma would offer their daughter to take a good-looking guy into their room? Unless, that said momma already knew that their daughter had no chance with that said good-looking guy, or that she could see he wasn't her type. Which he wasn't.

Of course, I could admire. Who wouldn't? But I found him...too prim and proper.

"Sure. Come on, Kane." I grabbed some books and left him to take the rest. He followed the couple of steps it took to get to my room. I didn't care that my room wasn't fancy, and I didn't care that Kane Stanley was about to see it. I was happy with how my room looked, and that was all that counted.

I should have known Momma had an ulterior motive to get me into my room.

"Barbra, guess what. Skylar has her history partner here, and my goodness, he is a fine young man," she said into the phone to her best friend Barbra Keating.

I groaned, shut my door, and quickly turned on my stereo to muffle the conversation going on in the kitchen.

I turned back to Kane, who was sitting at my desk, which lay under my window. He was laughing quietly.

"Yeah, laugh it up, mate. Wait until she starts on your case."

He sobered a little, but said, "Come on, it's a little funny.

I've never met an adult who would say 'blow-up doll' in front of me."

"Welcome to my world," I sighed.

With that, he glanced around my bedroom, taking in all that surrounded him. While he was busy, I got out my history book, tidied my desk a little so we could both fit, and sat down in the seat I pulled over from the other side of my bed, which I used as a bedside table.

"I'm guessing you're a fan of Ruby Gloom."

I took on an innocent voice and said, "Oh my, is it that obvious?" Of course it was. I had pictures of her and Skull Boy around everywhere. I even had a Ruby Gloom bed cover for my single bed, and figurines of all the characters from the show on my windowsill.

"By the way, what do you even know about it? I can't see you watching a show like that," I asked.

"My sister, who's five, loves it and tells me all about what's going on in Ruby Gloom's world."

"Now, she sounds like a nice girl."

"Why, because she watches the show?"

"Yeah." *Like, duh.*

"You seem to judge a book by its cover all the time, Sky," he said, shaking his head at me and starting to go through some books.

"Hey, I do not." I glared at him when he looked at me with his eyebrows raised. I rolled my eyes. "Okay, maybe I do. But come on, Kane, it's not hard. You can't tell me that Donna isn't a Barbie-type. She loves to shop. She loves makeup. She loves to talk about herself and to dress in name brands. She loves attention, and she definitely doesn't have a brain. And you can't honestly tell me that outside of this assignment, we would have ever talked, or that you would have ever approached me."

He sighed loudly. "You're right on some things—not that I'm saying you're right with anything you said about Donna. You don't really know her, so it's best not to judge her around me. But it's true; I wouldn't have spoken to you before this, but it's not like I felt I *could* either. You come across as a very stand-offish kind of person. Doesn't mean it can't change now."

I made my eyes go wide and put my hand to my heart. "Why, Kane Stanley, do you want to be besties with me?"

He rolled his eyes and turned back to his book, but he still couldn't hide the lip twitch, like he was trying to hold back laughter. I smiled to myself.

"I brought a heap of books from our library. I thought we could start from when they were young, and then move on to how they met and so forth. I'm sure one of these books should have most of the information; if not, I'm sure we can Google it. What do you think?"

"Sounds like you've really thought it through. All right, I'll start with this pile; you take that one, and let's see what we can find."

It was about an hour later when Momma called that tea was ready. We seemed to have gotten a heap of notes separately. All we had left to do was share what we had and hope that it wasn't the same.

It felt strange having Kane in my room working silently by my side. Every now and then, I would glance over and watch him. Sometimes, I'd catch him in the process of doing the same with me; we both just smiled and continued working.

I thought it would have been awkward having him here, but it wasn't. I felt at ease with him, and that was just weird.

"Come on," I said, "before she comes in here and drags us out by the ear."

Kane laughed until I looked at him seriously. "She wouldn't really?" he asked.

It was my turn to laugh. "Oh, you better believe it."

Momma put the last plate on the table and smiled at us

both. I watched Kane look from one plate to another, realizing there were only two sets, but three of us in the house.

"Momma would have already eaten," I explained and sat down.

"That's right; now I must be off. Be a good girl for once, Skylar, or I'll tan your behind."

I smiled and shook my head at Kane, who still seemed confused.

"Momma works the night shift."

"You're here all alone?"

"Well, duh."

"And that does not mean you will share this information with any of your young men friends. I do not want any of them turning up here taking advantage of my Skylar," Momma said sternly.

"No, Mrs James. I would never."

"I knew I liked you. Such manners." To my embarrassment again, she gave us both a kiss on the forehead and went back to her room to grab her coat, only to appear again saying as she walked to the front door, "Don't stay up too late; you both have school tomorrow. Nice meeting you, Kane."

"You too, thank you again for dinner."

"My pleasure. Night all."

"Night, Momma."

"Goodbye, Mrs James."

I didn't wait for the door to close before I started digging into one of my favourite stews Momma cooked.

After a few seconds, Kane joined in and moaned on his first mouthful. "This is good."

"Yeah, Momma can do wonders with road kill."

His fork paused halfway to his mouth; his eyes were wide in horror. I laughed so hard I had to hold my stomach.

"I'm jesting, Kane. Oh, God, you should have seen your face."

"Funny-ha-ha. I really don't know what's going to come out of your mouth sometimes."

"All the better to surprise you with, my dear," I said in an old lady's voice. He looked at me strangely. "Oh, come on; you know, *Little Red Riding Hood*, when she says to the wolf who's in disguise as her grandmother, 'Oh, granny, what big ears you have,' and the wolf replies with, 'All the better to hear you with, my dear.' You know, right?"

"Uh, no."

"Seriously? I love that story. I used to act out the wolf part. I always wished he'd eaten her. I mean, how stupid can you get, thinking the wolf could be her grandmother?"

Kane was smiling at me. "Trust you to like the wolf. I'll have a look at it one day."

"I'm surprised you haven't heard of it; didn't your parents used to read to you when you were young?"

He looked down at his food, his expression turning sombre. "No, they're always too busy, which is probably why Dommy watches so much television. I guess it's just lucky Mary is there to help with her homework, cooking, and other things."

Oh, boy, maybe things weren't always that great where money was concerned.

I couldn't stop my stupid hand. I placed it on his arm, and he looked down at it, then up at me. "Don't worry about it. I'll open the storytelling world to Dommy, and if you want to listen, I won't stop you."

He laughed. "I don't know whether to be grateful or scared."

"Probably both." I nodded.

We stayed on small talk throughout dinner, and when we'd finished, we still sat at the table talking about anything we'd think of. I had to admit, I was enjoying myself, but I knew once tomorrow came and I got on the bus, we'd go back to not knowing each other. Could you imagine what Donna would say if I walked to the back where they sat and finished the conversation about who's a better band: Nickelback, which was my favourite, or Linkin Park, who Kane liked, but I couldn't stand. All right, some of their songs were okay, but it wasn't like I would say that to him.

Donna would definitely freak, and really, I kinda think Kane would as well. Didn't matter to me; at least, I knew he wasn't as bad as I'd thought. Still, it wasn't like we'd hang with each other when all this finished. We'd go back to the way things were before this even started.

THREE

SKYLAR

It was Saturday morning and I was nervous. And because I felt nervous, I was annoyed with myself. I headed my way—by bus, of course—to Kane's place for more work on our assignment. I was right in thinking that nothing would change after having him at my house on Monday night; because it hadn't. I got on the bus the next day as normal, wearing my make-up, long black skirt, and a long sleeved, black-and-white striped top. He didn't say anything to me, and didn't even wave as I thought he might have. Truth be told, I didn't even glance to the back of the bus in his direction to see if he had done anything to acknowledge my presence.

Though, Wednesday I was standing at my locker with Javis, who was looming over me with one hand next to my head. We were talking about plans for the weekend, when out the corner of my eye, I spotted Kane and some of his mates walking down the hallway in my direction. I could have stabbed my heart when it picked up speed. I was trying my best to concentrate on Javis as Kane grew closer and closer.

"Hi, Sky." I heard. I looked over Javis's shoulder and gave a small wave.

Javis started laughing. "Now I know why you aren't listening to a thing I say, and why you just agreed to be my lover."

I looked up to him. "No way would I say that. No offense, Javis, you're..."

I stopped when I heard one of Kane's friends say, "Why would you talk to something like that? She's feral."

"Excuse me?" Javis growled. He turned to face Dale Quiall, the one who had said it.

"Javis, don't." I grabbed his arm quickly.

"You got something you want to say to me?" Dale hissed and glared back at Javis.

"Dale, just leave it. Come on or we'll be late for practice," Kane said, and then walked off. Dale soon followed.

Javis sighed, turned back to me, and said, "Now that's why it's best to steer clear of their kind. Jerks, that's all they are and ever will be."

"Yeah, I know." It wasn't as though I wanted to hang with them or anything...and Kane was the one who said hi to me. So that made Kane not as bad as the others, right?

Thursday, I had History again, only when I got in there and sat down next to Kane, an announcement over the PA called him away to an important football meeting. He apologized and said he'd see me Saturday, leaving a piece of paper on the desk with his address, home phone number, and mobile. I folded it back up and placed it in my backpack.

So there I was, at 11 Derves Drive, standing in front of a mansion.

"You have got to be kidding me," I muttered.

And he came to my house. Should I apologize for that? Probably, from the looks of what stood in front of me. I would have walked up the long driveway to the, I think, three-story, brick, elegant monstrosity, but the iron gates stopped that. I looked to my left; they had one of those intercomy-thingies. I really hated those; I hated speaking into them or answering machines, and I hated people hearing my voice on the other end. Still, I didn't have a choice—another thing I hated.

I walked over to it and pressed the bottom, then stood waiting for an answer.

"Si?" A lady's voice rang out from the tiny box.

I bent and pressed the button to talk back, "Yeah, hi. I'm here to see Kane, we—ah, have to study," I said. I heard some kind of movement, and then noticed a camera sitting on top of the fence moving to stare down at me. *Great*, I sighed, *now, they definitely wouldn't let me in.* Maybe I should have gone with a more normal look instead of wearing my usual make-up, tight, black vinyl pants, and a long white shirt with a black vest over the top.

You could say I was surprised when the gate buzzed and started to open. I quickly moved through the small gap before they could change their minds. I was sure my heart beat faster the closer I got. I was worried I'd start to sweat as well. Then I would smell and totally look like a freak if my make-up ran. I had considered not applying it, mainly because of Kane's little sister. I didn't want to scare her, but then I thought if she watched Ruby Gloom, she couldn't be that bad. And really, if I was going to be around here a few times, she had to get used to me the way I was. That went for his mom and dad as well.

The double front doors opened before I could knock, and a little, middle-aged, plump lady stepped around it.

"Hola, soy, Rosita," she said, touching her chest.

"Hola, soy, Skylar." I smiled.

"Par favor, ven en Kane no pasara' mucho tiempo." She gestured for me to enter, so I did.

"Gracias, Rosita." I stood just inside the door, taking in everything I saw. In front of me stood a grand staircase that spiralled up to the next level. I glanced up and saw that there was another level above the second one. I looked to my left, but all I saw was the same as the right side. Beyond the staircase were closed wooden doors. So I turned back to Rosita, who was taking the opportunity to check me out. From the look on her face, she didn't like me one bit.

She stood to the side of me, arms crossed, and over her shoulder, her look was scolding. "Cuidar a un fantasma de beber?" she asked in Spanish.

I couldn't help but laugh. I was lucky enough to know Spanish; I loved the language. She had asked, 'Care for a drink, ghost one?' I smiled at her and said back in her own language, "I am no ghost, Rosita, just silly make-up. You do not need to worry. I will be on my best behaviour, just like my momma taught me."

Her eyes widened and then she laughed.

"I didn't know you could speak Spanish," Kane said as he descended the stairs.

"There are a lot of things you don't know, Kane," I said.

"I like this one, Kane," Rosita said in English, with a very heavy Spanish accent still present.

"I guess I passed the test?" I asked, smiling. She returned it with one of her own.

"Si, with flying colours. I must go and find Dominique. Despedida, Skylar."

"Si, despedida. Encantado de conocerte, Rosita." I had said, 'Yes, farewell. Nice meeting you, Rosita.' She gave me a warm smile and left to climb the stairs.

"You almost need an elevator in here," I commented.

"Almost," Kane said. He'd been quiet since arriving, so I looked over my shoulder to him; he seemed confused about something.

"Okay, so where are we doing this?" I asked, gesturing to the backpack I had full of heavy books on my back.

"Right, uh, let's go in here," Kane said, pointing to the room to the left. "I left most of the stuff I was going over in here last night." He opened the door and moved out of the way so I could walk in first. I couldn't stop the gasp. I was in awe. The room was a library, and it was beautiful and huge. The walls were stacked from top-to-toe with books; one of those sliding ladders stood against the far right wall. On the left, at the front of the house, was a ginormous bay window. I walked over to it and looked out to the large front yard—you could almost say paddock. The sun was shining. It was a nice warm day out there, but having the windows so big, it nearly felt like you weren't missing out. Honestly, I felt like something out of *Beauty and the Beast*, only I'd be the beast.

Kane cleared his throat behind me. I turned to find him sitting at one of the tables in the middle of the room.

"Sorry. It's just...like nothing I've ever seen before." I shook my head, walked over to the table, and sat opposite him. "Let's start then," I said, getting my things out of my bag that I had dumped on the floor when I walked in, but Kane must have brought it to the table.

"It's all right, I can understand if I was seeing it for the first time too." He smiled. I didn't bother saying anything, only nodding. "Sky, I—uh, I wanted to say sorry for the other day, you know, with Dale—"

"You don't need to apologise. You didn't say it, so just forget about it. Only..."

He raised his eyebrows at me, "Only what?"

"Like Javis said, there's never going to be anything between us." I pointed to me, and then pointed to him, "and you guys. We're too different; we don't get you and you don't get us." I shrugged. "There's no harm in it, but that's the way things are, and always will be."

"I'm not like them," he uttered.

"We'll see." I knew there'd be only an amount of time before pressure from his kind would put an end to how he'd been with me—nice.

We worked on our assignment for half an hour before his phone rang; he looked at the number, then at me. He went to place it back down on the table.

"You can answer it."

He picked it up. "This won't take a sec. Hi, babe."

Yay, just what I wanted to hear, a smoochy conversation between the two of them.

He cleared his throat and said into his phone, "No, not right now; I'm kind of busy." I rolled my eyes without him seeing as he started to walk to the door saying, "What am I doing? I—uh, I have to help out with Dommy..."

That was all I heard before he disappeared into another room. So she didn't know I was here. That didn't surprise me. I could think of the many reasons why he wouldn't tell her.

I tried to continue with the work, but I couldn't concentrate. What was he telling her?

Turning to the door, I saw movement and found a young, pretty, girl-version of Kane standing there, half-hidden by the door.

"Hi. Dommy, isn't it? I'm, Skylar, but you can call me Sky." I gave her a smile. Still, she didn't move or say anything. "Hey, what are you up to? Me, you ask? I have to study with your boring brother; what a pain, huh? Wish I could be doing something else, like watching my all-time favourite show *Ruby Gloom*."

I heard her suck in a breath. "You like *Ruby Gloom?*" she asked, suddenly interested enough to take a step into the library.

"Sure do. Skull Boy is so cute."

"I know, but I also love Frank and Len...and Scaredy Bat is so funny. Why do you wear that white stuff on your face?"

"I like it; reminds me of Misery."

She nodded. "Okay. Do you want to see all my figurines from *Ruby Gloom?*"

"Sure, I'd love to." I wrote a note on a piece of paper telling Kane I'd been kidnapped by some child, and placed it on his side of the desk. "Let's go." I smiled and followed her out the door.

Her room was on the second floor; she told me on the way there that the third floor was for her parents. She wasn't allowed up there because they had too many breakables. God, she was five, so she'd know by now what to touch or not, right?

She opened her door, and again I was in awe. If a child could have everything in the whole wide world, you'd only have to look in Dommy's room to see that was exactly what she had. There was a lot of floor space, but her walls were covered in shelves, and on most of those shelves was everything from dolls to remote control cars. It was good to see she didn't just stick to girly toys. But seriously, the cute, long, curly-haired girl had way too much stuff.

A feeling of sadness touched me because I could tell—from what I'd heard and from what I could see—that her parents were never around; in return, they bought her love and affection with objects.

Above her bed sat four shelves, and on those were all the figurines ever created of all the *Ruby Gloom* characters. Of course, I wouldn't deflate the girl, so I proclaimed how great they were while she explained each of them with excitement showing in her eyes.

"Would you play Barbies with me?"

I had to do a double take. Did she really ask me, *me* to do that? I had never been a Barbie person. But how could I say no to those cute, pleading Bambi eyes.

"Sure, but just for a little bit though."

She squealed and ran to her closet, pulling a huge container out from within.

I was sure it had been a long, slow hour, until I looked at my watch and it told me only fifteen minutes had passed. I could not go on like this much longer.

I had pretended to be Ken, Barbie's boyfriend. I had taken her pets for a walk, and then I was Barbie's best friend, who was helping Barbie choose something to wear for her outing.

I was looking through Barbie's clothing when I asked, "Doesn't she have anything black?" I was a bit frustrated. Everything Barbie owned was so bright, it could almost make someone sick.

"No, silly." Dommy laughed, shaking her head at me. Then she stopped and looked at me seriously. "You know what?"

"What?" I smiled.

"You're so much better than Donna. I think Kane should be your boyfriend, not hers. She's mean and never plays with me."

I really didn't know what to say to that.

"Hey, squirt."

I spun my head to see Kane grinning and leaning against the doorframe.

"Kane," Dommy screamed and ran to him, climbing up his body and into his arms.

Thankfully, he wasn't here a few seconds ago to hear what Dommy just admitted to me.

I looked up at Kane, who was looking back; I shrugged my shoulders and held up one of Barbie's pieces of clothing, frowning. "No black; it's a tragedy."

He laughed and put Dommy back on her feet, who ran back over and hugged me. I was too shocked to do anything at first, but then wound my arms around her.

"I know you have to go study with my boring brother, but..."

"Hey." Kane feigned being hurt.

"What? That's what *she* called you." Dommy pointed at me. I snorted at her honesty; Kane raised his eyebrows. I shrugged and turned my attention back to Dommy, who said, "Can you come back and play another day?"

"I would love to. And maybe next time I'll bring a few books with me and I'll read them to you."

She squealed, gave me another hug, and then went back to playing. I got up and walked over to the door.

"You are full of surprises," Kane said.

"Yeah? Well, I guess you could say that." I smiled and walked back down to the library, with Kane silently following me.

"Sorry about the call and you having to play with Dommy."

"She's cute." I laughed. "Hey, any chance we can restart again Monday? It's just that I have to meet the others soon at the fair." I was actually late. I was supposed to be at the air by two, and it was already four.

"Sure, I was the one who wasted our time. So you're going to the fair?"

"That's what I said."

"I might see you there later. I'm meeting..."

I laughed at him. "Yeah, just don't say hi so Javis won't have to defend me." Something crossed his face; I wasn't sure what emotion it was, but it was gone too quickly to decipher.

"Sorry, again."

I rolled my eyes. "You don't have to be. Look, I may see you later; if not, catch ya Monday, okay?"

"Yes. Have a nice time, Sky."

"You too, Kane." I waved and left him standing in the library.

FOUR

SKYLAR

I had to wait for another bus at the corner of Kane's street, which made me another half-hour late to meet my friends at the fair. I hadn't expected them to wait for me out front; we'd already set the rules that if someone was late, then that person would have to suffer and search the whole fair for the others. Which was reasonable, except I hadn't thought it would be me. So there I was, walking around the fair for the last twenty minutes on my own, looking like a fool. I couldn't believe I hadn't found them yet, you would think that my friends would stick out like a sore thumb, but apparently not.

I turned the corner into the food area and ran right into Kane. He was standing with a drink in his hand at the time, which I knocked and ended up spilling it all over the person standing next to him—Donna.

"Watch where you're going, loser! Now look at me!" she cried.

There were only a few spots on her designer jeans and high heels—Kane must have just about finished it—and really, who would want to wear high heels to a fair for God's sake. The answer was right in front of me.

"Donna," Kane said with a tone of warning.

Yeah, like she'd listen.

"What? Look what she's done. We might as well go home," she whined and stormed off.

Pleasant as always.

"Sorry, Skylar, she's not always like that."

I rolled my eyes and snorted. "It's all right, Kane. At least I'm not the one going out with plastic-head." Damn it, I promised Momma I wouldn't do that. "Sorry, I shouldn't have said that. You'd better catch up to her before she gets hysterical and breaks a nail. Stuff it, sorry." He didn't seem that concerned; at least he was smirking.

"Hey, Princess Puff Cake," I heard Mitch yell. I looked across the food area and found my friends coming our way, only Massie was missing.

"Princess Puff Cake?" Kane asked, amused.

"Really, don't ask." I smiled. "Hi, guys, where the heck have you been? And where's Massie?"

The guys eyed Kane warily. Jessie openly ogled him. It was Javis who answered, "She couldn't make it, I guess. She didn't turn up out front, like you. What kept ya?"

"A cute five-year-old," I replied. "You guys know Kane, right?"

"Sure, how you doing, man?" Mitch asked.

"Good," he replied. And then silence fell among us; it felt awkward. Kane cleared his throat and we all turned to him. "Ah, have you guys been on all the rides?"

"Oh, yeah. Well, all the scary ones. Jessie here, of course, opted out, but now that Princess is here, we'll get to do it all over again." Mitch gleamed.

"I went on the pirate ship once. Never again. Bad memories. The guy in front of me had drunk too much and ended up puking, which landed right in my face." Kane shuddered from the memory.

"Gross, man. Reminds me of the time..."

They—as in the guys—ended up telling each other sick

stories about things that had happened to them. Jessie and I stood back and watched the three of them bonding; it was good to see.

"He is so hot," Jessie whispered to me, as the three of them doubled over laughing about when Javis had shaved his brother's eyebrows off one night, and super-glued rhinestones in their place.

I screwed my nose up at her. "He's okay."

"Kane!" A banshee screeched.

Kane winced. We all looked behind us and saw Donna standing a few feet away, fuming.

"Ah, man, you're in trouble," Javis sang.

"Catch you guys later." Kane drew his brows together.

Before he could take off, Mitch said, "Hey, you're not a bad guy. Any time you want to hang, feel free."

"Thanks." He smiled, gave them a chin lift, and ran off.

"That was nice of you, Mitch." Jessie smiled.

"It can happen every now and then. So, what ride do you want to go on first, Sky?"

"All of them, of course."

"You're as bad as the guys. Why am I friends with you again?" Jessie teased, placing her arm through mine as we walked off to the nearest ride.

"Probably because I put up with you."

An hour later, I was lined up for the last ride—the Ghost House. I knew it'd be as lame as always, but I couldn't leave here unless I'd been on it, and this was the only ride Jessie was willing to go on that night. Jessie and I went to sit next to one another until Mitch gave me the stink eye. Javis came over saying he'd sit next to me in case I got too scared and needed a big strong man for support. We both laughed it off, and Jessie went willingly to sit in a carriage beside a beaming Mitch.

I was right about the lameness; Javis and I laughed through the whole thing. What was funnier for us was that we could hear Jessie squealing behind us in her two-seated carriage with Mitch.

She may come across as one of the most fearsome girls in school, but then all you'd have to do was jump out and scare her, and she'd be hidden in a corner.

"Man, that keeps getting worse every year." Javis laughed.

"Poor Jessie will be comatose." We waited near the exit for their carriage to come out, and when it did, Javis and I doubled over laughing. I swear, if Jessie wasn't wearing her Goth make-up, she'd be just as white as the powder on her face. Her eyes were wide with fright; she had her arms securely wrapped around Mitch's arm, and if she could, she'd be sitting in his lap. Which wouldn't bother Mitch one bit.

Mitch held out his hand to help her out of the carriage. She quickly got up and out, and even though she walked our way with her head held high, I knew she was still feeling put out by the ride because she still hadn't let go of Mitch's hand.

"You all right, chicky?" Javis asked while trying to keep a straight face.

"Yeah, fine." She nodded.

"Uh-huh," I added, smiling at her.

"Oh, shut up, you two," she growled, which made us laugh again.

"You were fine." Mitch comforted her by swinging his arm around her shoulders, only this time, she didn't playfully push him away.

"Anyway, I'm starved," Javis said, rubbing at his stomach.

"When aren't you?" Jessie glared.

"Who wants? My shout," he called over his shoulder, walking off to the food area.

"Oh, in that case, I'll have a soda and a hot dog," I said. Mitch and Jessie declined. We watched Javis stop to stand in the long waiting line.

"Hey," I heard from behind me. I turned to find Kane standing there.

"Hi, what are you doing back?" I asked, the surprise showing in my voice.

"I'm meeting up with some of the guys, but I spotted you first. Hi, Jessie, Mitch," he added. They looked over from their own conversation and replied a greeting.

"So are you saying I stand out like this?"

"No—I. No, I'm not saying that." He actually blushed.

I bumped his shoulder with mine. "I'm teasing, Kane. I know I do."

As if to prove my point, someone called out my name. I looked over Kane's shoulder to find Josh Hill standing a few feet away.

"Josh!" I squeaked. He came over and pulled me into a big, warm hug.

"God, how long has it been?" he asked, pulling back from the embrace. "You look the same, well, besides the—" He gestured to the make-up.

"Yeah, it's a phase I'm going through." I blushed.

"Looks good on you."

"Thanks. So what are you doing back?"

I hadn't realized Kane had moved away until I heard him behind me, asking Jessie or Mitch, "Who's that guy?"

"A boyfriend Sky had when she was fifteen, but he moved away."

Not just any boyfriend. Josh was the one I thought I was in love with and would have given my virginity to. That was until his parents decided to move to another state and my heart broke. He still looked the same, still tall, slim, but well formed, with short, dark brown hair and eyes, chiselled cheek bones, and nice pouty lips.

Nearly as good as Kane.

Wait, where had that thought come from? It was true though; Kane was a very good-looking fella. He was the same height as me, well built, not skinny, but not overly huge. He was a darker blond than his sister, which he wore in that popular messy look, having it fall in his deep sea blue eyes.

"I'm back here to live." Josh smiled. My heart raced.

"Oh, uh, that's good. Um, do you remember Jessie?" I asked, turning around to face the others.

"How could I forget Jessie? You two were glued to each other's side." He smiled. But there was something else there, only I couldn't put my finger on it.

"Yeah, we still are." Jessie gave a forced smile.

"Uh, this is Mitch." He was still standing next to Jessie with his arm slung over her shoulder. "And this is Kane."

Josh raised his eyebrows and asked, "Boyfriend?"

"No, no, never. Just a…friend."

"Cool, nice to meet you," Josh said, holding his hand out to Kane. Kane went to take it until someone behind Josh called out his name. A girl-someone, who was very beautiful.

"I better go; that's…a cousin. Nice seeing you, Skylar."

"She prefers Sky," Kane supplied. I glared at him. Mitch and Jessie started laughing.

"Right, that's right. Anyway, I guess I'll see you around; seems I'll be starting back at school on Monday."

"Okay. I'll see you there."

He gave me one last hug, which lingered a little longer than before, and left.

I turned back to the others, not able to control my smile. Josh Hill was back in town. Would we take off where things had been between us? A girl could hope.

"Wow, that was Josh," I smartly said.

"Never liked the guy," Jessie said.

"I don't think I will either," Kane added.

"What the hell, you guys? First, Jessie, you have never said anything to me about it before, and second, Kane, you're just worried he'll take over the spot as 'most popular guy at school', because he likes football...and he's so good looking."

Kane glared at me. "Yeah, that's it, Sky. But I know he won't stand a chance."

"Oh, go and cry to your Barbie," I retorted, and felt bad right after saying it. He started to walk off. "Kane, Kane, wait.

I'm sorry; I shouldn't have said that." I grabbed his arm to stop him.

He turned, grabbed my shoulders, and kissed me. It was only a short kiss, but God almighty, I felt it right down to my toes. Imagine if he had used tongue...

"And I shouldn't have done *that*," he said, and continued to walk off.

I was in too much shock to stop him.

"Oh. My. God," Jessie screamed.

No, I couldn't think about that. I wouldn't. *Why did he do that? He has a girlfriend. Was it to prove some point that I will never get? How dare he! He has no right to get me all confused, worried, and mixed up. He doesn't know me. I don't know him. Why did he do that? HE has a girlfriend.* The thoughts circled again. The frigging ass-pig who had nice sweet-soft lips.

"I think she's gone into shock," Mitch said.

I hadn't seen them walk over to me, but Mitch was waving a hand in front of my face.

"Sky, honey? Sky, come back to us now," Jessie said while she shook me.

"That stupid, self-righteous prick! How dare he do that to me? He can't do that; he has a plastic girlfriend! I am going to beat the hell out of him for doing that, for confusing me, making me think..."

"That you want him to do it again?" Jessie offered.

"Damn it, yes. That asshole. Still, it will never happen again. Josh is back; things can go back to how they were. Kane and I will finish this assignment, and then he can go back to his perfect little plastic life. Then...yeah, then I'll live happily ever after with Josh."

"God, I hope not," Jessie mumbled.

"What did you say?" I asked, knowing perfectly well what it was. What did she have against Josh. And what did she think of what Kane had just done? I wanted to ask her, but then again, I didn't want to talk about it.

"Nothing. Nope, nothing at all," Jessie said.

Javis came up beside us. "Okay, what have I missed?" he asked.

"Kane turned back up. Josh—Sky's old boyfriend—came and got her thinking that there may be something between them still. Then Josh left, Kane cracked it over something, and Sky was rude to him. Nothing new from our girl there. Then he was walking off, Sky apologised, and Kane kissed her. And now she doesn't know where she's at," Mitch explained.

"Crap, now I definitely don't have a chance," Javis said.

Eyes wide, I looked over to him as he shrugged and bit into his hot dog. Yeah, and he really looked broken up about it...*not*. I rolled my eyes, grabbed my soda and hot dog, and hoped that food would take away any thoughts of what just happened.

Notice how I said *hoped*.

FIVE

SKYLAR

Walking into History on Monday was harder than I thought it would be. I was a bundle of nerves. I tried to keep my heart and stomach from fluttering, or from thinking about Kane's lips upon mine. All I wanted to do was take back what had happened. I hated the way I was feeling.

And it was *his* entire fault.

I glared down at Kane and then sat quietly next to him; he didn't meet my gaze, not that I expected him to. The teacher came in and told us to start working, so I leaned over and grabbed my books out of my bag. When I straightened up, there was a piece of paper on my side of the desk. I knew it was from him—*eye roll*—who else would it be from? I also knew that it would be a note saying sorry, that he shouldn't have done it. Well, true, he shouldn't have, especially when he had a girlfriend who was sitting in the back of the room.

Though, I didn't want an apology. I hated the thought that he would be sorry for kissing me. So I screwed up the note and left it on his side of the table. I then proceeded to look through a book I'd placed on my desk while saying, "All right, what we have so far is all about the Roosevelt's younger years, so I went to the library yesterday," *to keep myself busy*, "and found some other information that I think we should add in. Then we can move on to their years at school and so forth."

He didn't say anything, and I'd finished flicking through the book, so I had to turn to look at him.

Letting out a loud sigh, he nodded.

The rest of the period, we worked. We stayed focused on what we had to get done and that helped. By the end, when the bell rang, we'd managed to get a lot done. I started packing up the books just as he was doing the same.

"Sky, I—"

"Come on, babe, let's get out of here; I'm starving." Donna had come up beside our desk, placing her hand on Kane's shoulder.

"Sure." Kane smiled up at her and stood. "See you later," he directed to me. I waved him off.

I waited for the coast to clear before heading out into the hallway. Mitch jumped out of nowhere, making me scream. I had forgotten he was even in the same class.

"Mitch, you do that again and I will kill you."

He laughed and slung his arm around my shoulders. "So, how did that go?"

I knew what he meant, my spending time with Kane after, well, that tiny, meaningless kiss.

"Fine, we're all about the assignment."

"You okay, P.P.?" He really sounded concerned.

"Yeah, don't stress about me. What you need to worry about is Jessie's new history partner." I rang her on Sunday to find out who it was after totally forgetting about it.

Mitch laughed. "Who? Avery Mack? No, I don't think I have to be worried there."

"Why? He's a great looking guy."

"Yeah, but I informed Jess that he bats for the other team."

I shook my head. "Mitch, don't you think after knowing Jessie for some time now that she may bring that fact up in front of him."

"Crap, I didn't think of that." He shrugged. "I guess I'll worry about it when it happens. Come on; let's go make ourselves sick on food."

"You read my mind."

We walked into the cafeteria and went straight up to the food counter. I grabbed chips and a hamburger, not forgetting a soda to wash it all down. I turned and started for the table, only to do a double take because sitting at our table, was Josh. My heart skipped a beat. I was actually happy to see him. He was the distraction I needed.

"Hey, guys." I smiled, sitting down next to Josh, who was sitting next to Javis. Jessie and Massie were on the other side, and Mitch quickly sat down next to—no brainer there—Jessie, who wasn't looking very happy today. I wondered what was wrong with her.

"Hi." Josh smiled back.

"How's the first day back?" Mitch asked.

"Totally weird, but I wouldn't have it any other way," Josh said while looking at me.

"Man, I can't believe I don't remember you from before," Javis said with a mouthful of hot dog—*really, another one?*

"I can." Massie smiled over at him.

"It was two years ago and I wasn't in your year, so I guess I can be forgettable. So what are the plans for the weekend?"

"Not much. Every second weekend we usually have a DVD night—*crap*, girl! What the hell was that for?" Javis glared at Jessie. She must have kicked him under the table.

"Whose house is it this weekend?" Massie asked.

"Mine," I said. "So I get to choose, and no bitchin' about what I get." I eyed Mitch and Javis, while using a chip to point at them. Josh leaned over and bit it out of my hand. I blushed. Not that he would have seen because of my make-up.

Josh held my gaze for what seemed like ten minutes, but was really only a few seconds, and then he looked away and leaned back in his chair, placing his arm on the back of mine. His fingers barely brushed my back, but I felt it. Goose bumps rose on my arms. Then my stupid brain wondered what sort of reaction my body would have if it had been Kane. I shook my head and concentrated on my food as the conversation went on around me.

The rest of the day went too fast, and before I knew it, I was home worrying about Kane coming over. I would have liked to cancel. I walked into the kitchen and spotted a note on the table, it read:

Hi, honey,

I've gone shopping but I'll be home soon. Kane called and said he went home sick from school early today, so he won't be able to make it tonight. Too bad! I would have liked to see his cute face. (Haha) xo

Now that just made me mad. I knew he wasn't sick; he just didn't want to be alone with me.

Was he too scared I'd try and jump his bones after that one little kiss. No, I wouldn't even call it that. It was a peck if anything.

How dare he ditch me! Fine, if he wanted to play it that way, then I could do the same. I'd just skip class on Thursday. Have him think that I didn't want to see *him,* or that I didn't want to spend time with him. And maybe I'd just forget about Saturday as well. That'd show that little skunk.

I did just what I'd said I would and skipped class on Thursday, under Jessie's disgust. Which she told me on Tuesday, after I explained my plan to her. She also mentioned that ever since Josh had been sitting at our table, she'd been watching Kane, and it was clear he didn't like what he was seeing. Especially when Josh would gently touch my cheek, or place his hand on my thigh, or tuck my hair behind my ear.

I laughed her off and told her I didn't care what he was

doing. Honestly, I was enjoying the attention from Josh, and I told her to give up the idea that Kane was interested in simple little old me. Because if that had been the case, he wouldn't be dodging me like he was, and he wouldn't have a girlfriend.

Instead, I noticed when he saw me coming down the hall, he'd choose to walk the other way. Didn't he think that would hurt? Well, it didn't.

I. Didn't. Care.

After coming down from my little rant and rave with Jessie, Friday night over the phone—about the way he was dodging me —I decided all this was silly. I had Josh—not officially—and Kane had Donna. So why couldn't we just work on the stupid assignment, get it done, and be on our merry way? That was when I decided I was going to Kane's house the next day. We still had a lot to get done, and if we couldn't work together, we'd both fail, and I was sure both of us didn't want that.

Standing out the front of his place ready to ring the intercom, I had second thoughts...until the gates opened. Someone must have seen me—*sigh*. I was walking up the driveway when the front door came flying open and a little blonde-headed monster came running out. I quickly held out my arms and braced myself, ready for the impact. Who would have thought such a tiny thing could have nearly knocked the breath out of me?

"Hey, Dommy, how're you doing?" I asked, planting her feet back on the ground after a big hug.

"Great now! Kaddy said you probably wouldn't come."

"He doesn't know what he's talking about. Hey, Dommy, how come you call Kane 'Kaddy'?" I asked, ruffling her hair as we made our way into the house, hoping to get some dirt that I could use later.

She giggled. "'Cause he was the one to start my name Dommy, so I called him Kaddy."

Well, that wasn't gonna give me much...if anything, it was —sweet."

"Hola, Skylar," Rosita said, coming from the room to my left.

"Hola, Rosita, how are you?" I asked in her own language.

She smiled and answered back in Spanish, "Can't complain because nobody would listen. It is good to see you here again."

"Thank you. Is Kane around?"

"I will call him." Rosita moved to the wall to speak into the intercom.

"Don't worry, Rosita, I'm here," Kane called out in Spanish as he descended the stairs. "I wasn't expecting you this morning," he said to me.

"Have you made other plans?"

"No."

"Well then, let's get to work." I started for the library until Dommy grabbed my hand.

"Can I come in too? I promise I'll be quiet; I'll play with my toys."

"Sure, sweetie. You go and grab them. And then later, I brought a book that I'm going to read to you," I said, patting my backpack. She beamed and ran off to her room to collect some toys.

"That is very nice of you, Skylar," Rosita said in English. "Isn't it, Kane?"

"Yes, it is."

I shrugged and moved to the library. I opened the door to see the table was already scattered with books. I went over and noticed that it was stuff from our assignment.

"So, you're feeling better?" I asked while tidying up the books so I could have room for my own.

"Fine, thanks...Skylar, I want to..."

"Don't," I hissed. I looked up from the table into his eyes. "Don't say sorry for doing what you did. The thought of you wanting to apologise and regretting it makes me angry. I know it shouldn't have taken place. Besides the fact you have a girlfriend, we're just too different. We both have our separate lives. So let's just forget the whole thing. We can finish this assignment, and then we can go back to the way things should be." I had to look away. Damn it, for some silly reason I felt like crying.

He took a breath; I didn't want to hear whatever he had to say. Thankfully, I was saved from hearing anything when Dommy came bouncing into the room, her arms full of Barbies.

We sat down at the table, Kane and me at one end and Dommy at the other. Kane and I spoke about what needed to be done, and with time, I started to relax. I think what helped was Dommy being there. Every now and then, she would come up and ask me for help to undress or redress one of her Barbies. I did it without thinking and kept the conversation going with Kane at the same time. After the second time of her coming up, she no longer asked for help; I just held out my hand and she'd place one of her dolls in it.

Two hours later, I called it quits. I wanted to head home to spend some time with Momma before she went into work, because then I'd have to get ready for the movies. Jessie had mentioned on the phone last night that we should actually go to the cinema to see one of the latest movies, instead of watching the same things over and over on DVD.

But first, I promised a certain little monster that I would read to them.

"All right, Dommy, where do you want me to read to you?"

"Oh, in my room, please."

Kane laughed at her excitement. "I'll finish this; you had better start before she bursts something."

Nodding, I followed Dommy out and to her room.

I was halfway through the book, with Dommy sitting as close as she could get next to me on her bed, when Kane appeared in the doorway. I didn't stop reading. I was on a roll and getting to the good bit. I felt him enter the room, come over to Dommy's bed, and then lay down behind us. I glanced quickly behind me to see him stretching out his body and placing his arms behind his head as he smiled up at me.

I rolled my eyes and continued. "Ready, Dommy? This is the best part. 'Why, Grandmother, what big eyes you have,'" I said in a little girl's voice. Kane laughed behind me. I turned to punch him in the stomach and went on, "All the better to see you with, my dear," I said in a gruff, deep voice, and again, Kane laughed.

"Shush, Kaddy," Dommy scolded. He shook his hands out in front of him, as if to say he'd be good.

Yeah, I'd believe it when I saw it.

I cleared my throat and began again, "Why, Grandmother, what big ears you have. All the better to hear you with, my dear." I turned the page. Kane sat up to look over my shoulder at the book, and then he ever so gently moved my hair out of the way by tucking it behind my ear. If it was Josh, I would have been fine, but with Kane, that small touch took my breath away.

"Kane, stop it; you're distracting her," Dommy cried. I blushed.

"Sorry again, squirt."

I had to clear my throat again. "Why, Grandmother, what big teeth you have. All the better to *eat* you with. The wolf dove out of bed to chase Little Red Riding Hood around Grandmother's house. Just when he was about to catch her and gobble her up, the door burst open, and there stood the woodcutter. With one strike of his axe, he cut the wolf's head off and saved the day. Then they both heard movement coming from the cupboard, so they went over to it and opened it carefully, and there was Little Red Riding Hood's grandmother safe and sound. The end." I closed the book and placed it down on the bed. "Well, what did you think?" I stared down at Dommy.

"I think you are the best reader in the whole wide world. Isn't she, Kaddy?"

"Yeah, especially with those voices." He laughed.

I glared. "The book's only good when you do it like that."

He smiled, but it quickly faded and he sat there just staring at me. I wanted to look away, but I didn't. He reached his hand out and ran the back of it against my cheek. My breath hitched from the touch. Shivers coursed through my body. I felt sick because I wanted more than just that small touch.

Why did he get my blood boiling? Was it because I couldn't have him? Was this some game to him?

I quickly stood and backed away from the bed. "I—uh..." I didn't know what to say to him, so I turned to Dommy. "I have to go now, but I'm sure I'll be back next Saturday, and maybe one day you can come to my house and I'll show you all the books I have. I'm sure your brother can drop you off."

"I'd love that!" she squealed. "Oh, Kaddy, do you think Mommy will let me?"

"We can only ask, squirt."

"All right, so I'll see you." I waved, turned, and just about ran out of the room and house.

SIX

SKYLAR

Saturday afternoon I spent with Momma watching an old video of *Calamity Jane*. It was a sing-song, corny movie, but that didn't matter; I enjoyed the time I spent with her. Until, she thought it was time for another sex-protection talk. She'd heard down the street yesterday that Josh was back in town. She knew how much it had hurt when he'd moved away in the first place.

"Have the two of you gotten back together?" she asked as we sat on the couch together.

"No, Momma. He's only been back a week." I pointed out.

"Doesn't matter. Things can happen fast when two people have feelings for one another."

My mind went straight to thinking of Kane, though I quickly squished those thoughts.

"Even though I still think there could be something between you and the good-looking Kane." She smiled when I rolled my eyes at her. "I know, I know, he has a girlfriend. All I want to say is when the time comes, I want you to feel comfortable to come to me and say, 'Momma I would like to go and see a doctor about birth control.'"

"Momma," I barked.

"No, sweetheart, you have to be prepared for when you

think the time does come. When you're with a guy, they will try to pressure you into bed, but I can only hope that you will wait until you think you're ready and have found the right guy to share that special moment with. All I am trying to get across is when you *are* ready, we will go and see a doctor together. Because the last thing I need is to be a grandmother when I'm still so young and beautiful." She flipped her hair over her shoulder. We both started laughing.

"I love you, Momma."

"I know, sweetheart, and right back at you." She smiled, giving me a quick hug as someone knocked on the front door. Momma carried our plates to the kitchen as I went to open the door.

My eyes widened when I found Josh standing there, looking great in a pair of light-denim jeans and a plain black tee.

"Surprise." He smiled wider.

"Hi, ah, do you want to come in?" I moved aside enough for him to enter.

He shook his head and gestured to the porch step. "I can only stay for a second, but can we talk out here? It's such a nice afternoon."

I stepped out and closed the door behind me, not before seeing Momma stick her head out of the kitchen and mouth '*Told you so.*' I shook my head, fighting a smile. I sat down next to him; he placed his arm around my shoulders.

"So, I wanted to...well, how 'bout I just show you?" He gently turned my head with his other hand and kissed me. When he deepened the kiss, I felt a spark of something— interest, maybe? Still, I felt as though there was something missing. It wasn't as though I didn't find him attractive, and it wasn't that the kiss had done nothing for me. But was it enough?

He pulled back and grinned down at me, and I found myself smiling back. I had wished for this for many years, to be reunited with the one I thought I lost forever. Although, now it was here, I didn't know what to think, or what I should be feeling.

But I knew the big gap of nothingness in the pit of my heart waiting for someone special was not a good sign.

"Well, I guess we can say let's take off where we left it two years ago?" he asked.

"I—ah, um. Yeah, I would like that." I needed to give this time. I wasn't missing out on something that could be great just because I had hopes for something that would never happen.

Josh made me smile, made me laugh, and I did have feelings for him. So maybe with time, they'd grow stronger.

"Great." He beamed and kissed me again. "I, um, I have to get going; my parents have organised this family thing and they'd kill me if I miss it."

"That's all right; we're going to have plenty of time together now." Even if those words freaked me out—a lot.

"True. I'll see you tomorrow, okay?"

"Sure."

He gave me one last peck, then left.

After he drove off, I opened the front door and went back inside, but I didn't get far. I closed the door and leaned against it, wondering if I had just done the right thing or if I was being mean to him. Was I leading him on?

"Oh, sweetie, you look so confused." Momma came over to give me a hug, and then pulled away, patting my back as she continued talking, "Everything will sort itself out in the end. And let me tell you, honey, there are plenty of fish in the sea, and if one of those fish doesn't float your boat, move on."

I snorted then laughed. "Momma, you're just full of advice today."

"That's what I'm here for, sweetie." She gave me a kiss on the forehead. "Now, I had better go and get ready for work; you never know, I may meet my prince charming tonight. So if I'm not home in the morning, then you know what happened."

"Yeah, and then you wake up."

She laughed. "And then I wake up."

Later that night, after Momma left for work, Jessie came around before we headed off to the movies. I'd washed my face and decided not to wear my Goth make-up. I didn't know about her, but my pores needed a break.

Maybe I should listen to my momma sometimes.

Though, Jessie talked me back into applying it, and nothing could take me away from my Goth gear, so I dressed in my red sneakers, red and black knee high socks, a very short, lace black skirt, with shorty-short black bike pants under it, and a tee that read 'A devil inside'. I had my medieval black and silver jacket to go over the top of my outfit in case I got cold. Jessie looked awesome in a hot pink and black corset, with a short-sleeved black jacket, three-quarter black pants, and biker boots. I asked her if she was trying to impress a certain someone; she smirked and said "maybe".

"Guess who came and saw me this afternoon," I said as we sat on the bus that would drop us right out in front of the movie theatre.

"Oh, oh, let me guess. Kane?"

"No," I said, rolling my eyes. "Josh. We're kind of dating again." I smiled. She didn't smile back or get excited for me.

"Really?"

"Yeah, why? Jess, what's your problem about him?"

"Sky, it's...nothing. Look, here's our stop." She stood before the bus stopped, nearly falling over when it came to a complete stop. I looked out the window and saw Javis, Massie, and Mitch already there waiting for us. Both Javis and Mitch wore jeans and tees, only Javis's tee was a dark blue, and Mitch's was a red. Massie was looking wonderful in a long, black, tight lacy dress and combat boots.

"Hey, guys." I smiled. Out the corner of my eye, I witnessed

Jessie and Mitch give each other a look, and then quickly turned away from one another.

"So, any idea what we're seeing tonight?" Javis asked as we walked into the theatre.

"That new Zombie movie looks good to me," I suggested.

"I am not going to see some scary show." Jessie pouted.

"Come on, girlfriend, that show rocks," Massie said. Javis and Mitch nodded in agreement.

"Right, we all vote. Zombies it is then." I smiled.

Jessie sighed and said, "I need knew friends."

"Come on, you love us." Mitch grinned, placing his arm around her shoulders, and she actually blushed.

"Let's go get the tickets."

"Wait, isn't that Kane over there?" Jessie said.

Those few words had my heart jumping out of my chest. I looked over my shoulder to where Jessie was pointing. It was in fact Kane, but standing with him was Donna. She wrapped her arms around his waist and kissed him on the cheek. I watched as his arm came around her and gently rubbed up and down her back.

"So it is. Come on or we're going to miss the movie," I said and started to walk off.

"Hi, Kane," Jessie yelled.

I could have killed her. Instead, I turned back around to see Kane walking our way with a reluctant Donna. It seemed he was dragging her our way by her hand.

"Hey, guys, what are you here to see?" he asked everyone, but looked at me.

"The new Zombie one," Javis supplied.

"That'd be a great movie. Donna, let's see that one instead."

Hell no, I thought, *I'm not sitting in a closed movie theatre with Kane making kissy-face at Donna.*

"No way! You promised we can see that Bridesmaids movie. That's the only reason I would be in here in the first place."

Donna pouted. Kane shook his head. Javis and Mitch covered their mouths to hide their laughs.

Massie coughed into her hand, saying, "Under the thumb." We all laughed, which caused Donna to glare at us. Still, at least Kane found it all amusing; he didn't seem fazed by any of it.

Kane ignored the whole comment and went on talking to the guys about other Zombie movies. Us girls stood by listening, and the only one who wasn't looking happy about it all was Donna. Was she worried we'd try to convert Kane over to the dark side?

"Oh, look, there's Josh," Jessie said. "No, wait, don't look, Sky."

Come on, when someone had said 'don't look', you had to then. I followed her gaze over to the food stand, and found Josh there with his tongue stuck down some girl's throat. The same girl he was with at the fair.

That was some family event he had to get to.

I felt pissed, annoyed, and embarrassed. Especially when Mitch asked what was going on and Jessie said, "Josh and Sky are supposed to be a couple as of this afternoon."

"No way," Javis uttered.

"That pig," came from Massie.

"I'll kill him for you," Mitch growled.

"Any wonder he chose her," Donna said quietly.

"Listen, cow, you do not diss my girl here, or you face me," Jessie hissed all up in Donna's face.

"Kane!" Donna squealed. Only he was nowhere to be found. She looked to her side, as we all did, and then looked around until we spotted him making his way over to the unsuspecting Josh. What was he going to do? Congratulate him or something for making a fool out of me?

We all watched as Kane tapped Josh on the shoulder. Josh turned and seemed surprised to see Kane standing there waiting for his attention. Kane said something, which made Josh look over his shoulder to me; his eyes widened, his mouth turning into an O-shape.

Kane was saying something else, but Josh was ignoring him. He shoved Kane out of the way and stomped over to me, with Kane on his tail.

Josh stopped right in front of me. "Sky, it's not what it looks like."

I couldn't help but laugh; how lame was that sentence? "Really, Josh? Wait, let me guess, she was choking on some popcorn and your tongue was the only thing that could save her." I put my hand to my heart. "Oh, Josh, how heroic of you."

My group laughed.

"No, look, I was going to end it with her tonight. I want you, babe. She's nothing anymore."

"What?" Apparently, the girl had followed them over here as well. I could see why Donna had said what she had. The girl was painstakingly beautiful. "Josh, I moved here for you and this is the way you treat me?" she cried.

"Yeah, Josh, you should be more careful. To think, you could have played us both. If I hadn't been here tonight, I wouldn't have found out."

Come to think of it, it did seem like this whole thing had been set up. I looked behind Josh to Jessie; she mouthed 'Sorry.'

She had known? Goddamn. She had some explaining to do.

"Joshy-boy, I think you'd better go," Javis suggested.

"No. Sky, come on, you know we'd be good together."

I shook my head at him and smiled. "I thought we could have, but now I know we won't. So, bye-bye, Josh," I said, waving with my hand in his face.

His worried expression turned into a scowl. He grabbed my hand with his own, forcing it down to his side. "No, we will be together." He started to walk off, and that was fine with me, only he hadn't let go of my hand, so I was now the one being dragged off.

"Let her go," Javis...no wait, Kane had said.

In the next second, Josh was tackled to the ground and Kane was standing over him. "If you ever come near her or speak to her again, I will find you and make you pay. Still, I think you should pay for hurting her in the first place."

Josh sprung up to stand in front of Kane, chest bumping him.

"Yeah, why? She isn't worth the trouble; the only reason I wanted to get back with her was because I thought she'd be easy. I mean, look at her; the way she dresses, it has easy written all over it."

Kane punched him in the face. Josh doubled over. Donna screamed as blood poured out of Josh's nose. Josh pretended to stand, but then tackled Kane around the waist, making them both fall to the floor. Josh sat on Kane and punched his shoulder, and Donna screamed again. I think everyone was in shock; we all just stood back as Josh and Kane wrestled and hit each other on the ground.

"Someone, stop him," Donna yelled.

I came out of my semi-coma and strode my way over to the two hooligans. By that time, Josh was on top of Kane again. I kicked Josh in the ribs and he rolled off coughing. *Must have done it pretty hard.* I smiled to myself. I bent over, grabbed Kane's hand, and helped him up; his right eye would probably be bruised, and his nose would definitely swell. I reached out to wipe away some of the blood, then Donna came hurling up and wrapped her arms around his neck.

"Oh, baby, are you okay?" she asked, planting a kiss on his cheek. She turned to me. "This is all you fault." She glared.

"You're right." I sighed and then turned to Kane. He didn't have to do that for me, but he did. Why? "Thanks, I guess. Sorry to ruin your pretty face." I smirked; he smiled back and shook his head. "Thanks again, though." He nodded.

I heard movement behind me and turned back to Josh, who was getting up from the floor holding his side. I went over to him, placed my hands on his shoulders, and kneed him in the spot I was always told never to hurt. He doubled over and then dropped to his knees.

"And that's for playing me. Don't worry about what Kane said. You should be more scared with what I would do to you first," I said and walked off.

Mitch, Massie, and Javis all cheered. Jessie smiled; she knew better than to talk to me right then. Kane and Donna had disappeared somewhere.

SEVEN

SKYLAR

After all the commotion Saturday night, I decided not to watch a movie; I'd had my fill of action for the night. Instead, I caught another bus home with Jessie, who asked to spend the night. Of course, I said yes, because she had some answers to give me. As Jessie lay on a mattress next to my bed where I was sitting, she sighed deeply and began explaining. The first thing she told me was that when Josh and I were going steady a couple years ago, he had approached her to see him behind my back. When she declined—by hitting him in the balls—he went straight for another girl from a different school. She found that out by catching him down the street one afternoon, then promptly told him that he was nothing but a piece of shit on the bottom of her shoe, and that he had better inform me what he'd been up to. He didn't, of course, because a couple of days after, his parents told him that they were moving.

I asked her why she didn't tell me herself. She snorted and informed me that I was so wrapped up in my tiny bubble of love that I wouldn't have believed her, which would have caused us to fight, ending our friendship. I had fallen silent, pondering all that she'd said, and in the end, I concluded that she would have been right. I would have done exactly that. We hugged. I forgave her, and then continued to ask her if she knew about Josh's new —old—whatever she was, girl, and if she'd known he was going to be there with her. She gave me one of her evil grins and nodded, saying that she'd overheard him on the phone with her, organising the movie date.

She wanted me to see for myself. I thanked her and told her to never do that again. From then on, she had to just tell me, and if I didn't believe her, she had permission to slap me and yell *Josh*. That made us both laugh.

She had asked me if I was upset about what happened with Josh. I told her the truth—that I was a little, but I didn't think my heart was really in it in the first place. She giggled and said it was because of Kane. I threw a pillow at her and told her to get stuffed. We both went on talking about what Kane had done for me in front of Donna. Which we knew would make Donna hate me even more. Jessie thought it had been very romantic. I scoffed, rolled my eyes, and told her I didn't want to talk about it anymore.

Sunday, Jessie left early. Momma came home and went straight to bed, complaining of a long, boring night and promising that when she woke later, we'd go out for pizza. Being left to myself in the house wasn't good. I didn't know how many times I went to reach for the phone to ring Kane to see how he was. But I soon talked myself out of it.

Monday morning, I walked into the kitchen to see Momma at the stove cooking; she turned to me and smiled.

"Kane rang while you were in the shower."

My heart started to fly. Damn heart.

"Yeah, what did he have to say?" I asked, trying to make myself sound bored.

"Just that he won't be at school today; his mother didn't think it best for him to be seen in public looking the way he does."

"Oh."

"How does he look, Skylar?"

"What makes you think I know?"

"You have that guilty look. What happened? Lord, please tell me you didn't dress him up in that gunk you call make-up?"

I laughed, shook my head, and then sobered. "No, Momma." I sighed. "You know how Josh and I got back together and that I went to the movies Saturday night with my friends?" She nodded. "Well, Kane and his girlfriend were there—"

"Oh God, does this end in you kicking her butt and Kane jumping in?"

I rolled my eyes. "No, Momma, if you just let me finish." She gestured with her hand. "So we were standing there talking, and then Jessie pointed out that Josh was there—"

"Oh, that's nice of him to turn up." She smiled.

"Momma, he had his tongue stuck down a girl's throat."

"That little asshat! My word, I'm going to talk to his Momma—"

"No, you can't. Just shush for a second. Kane went up to him saying he shouldn't treat me like that and they got in a big fight. Blood and guts—well, no guts actually, but blood, heaps of blood, pouring everywhere. I ended up breaking up the fight, and kicking Josh in the ribs and the balls. I thanked Kane. He disappeared with his girlfriend, and I came home with Jessie."

"Oh, my. Well, I do have to say you know how much I hate violence, but good for you girl for sticking him one. And Kane..." she gushed, "what a nice young gentleman. I knew I liked him for a reason."

"Why yes, Momma, isn't he just the best?" I said in my best southern accent and fluttered my eyelashes at her.

"No need for sarcasm, girl. You know you're not too young to be spanked."

"That is just wrong to say, Momma, on so many levels. Anyway, did Kane say anything else?"

"Oh yes, that he'll still be coming around tonight." She smiled.

Thankfully, I'd already applied my white powdered make-up to hide the blush creeping up my neck.

I made it through the day without Donna saying anything to me. Even though I could feel—many times— her cold, hard glare at the back of my head. At lunch, my friends could not stop talking about the fight, going through it play-by-play while I sat silently eating, smiling and nodding, or laughing when I had to.

Finally, the day ended. I hadn't seen Josh all day—probably hiding his wounded pride. I wondered what he'd told people if they asked.

At home, I found Momma in the kitchen dressed in her work uniform and busy cooking dinner. I watched her for a while, humming to the radio that sat on the counter beside her, playing some country and western song I didn't know. She swayed her hips while cutting up the potatoes.

"Nice moves, Momma." I smirked.

She glanced over her shoulder and stuck her tongue out. "Sod off, you rotten child."

How very grown up she was. She was actually thirty-five, but acted and even looked like she was still in her twenties. Men still gawk at her when she'd be walking down the street. I knew from witnessing it with my own eyes. I kept telling her she could have any guy she wanted, and then she'd inform me that she was waiting for her special man to turn up and sweep her off her feet. Then she continued about how one day I would find my own special man and be swept away.

"How was your day anyway, child of mine?" she asked as I helped myself to a coke.

"Same, same. How long 'til tea? I want to get in a shower."

"You have half an hour and I've made enough for you and Mr Kane. Or did you forget he is coming by tonight?" It was then she smirked and started laughing. "Of course you wouldn't. Well, run along and get that disgusting stuff off your face."

"You know, sometimes I wonder who the witch is in this

family." I ducked as she threw a carrot at me, and bolted for the shower.

I was just getting dressed when I heard a knock at the front door. He was early; I quickly jumped into some black tracksuit pants and a long-sleeved, striped, black and grey top. At the same time, I did my best to ignore the butterflies discoing in my stomach.

I really had to stop that...somehow.

Pulling the towel off my hair, I heard a squeal come from the front of the house. I realised it was Momma, and then she said, "Oh, who do we have here?"

Maybe it wasn't Kane after all.

"Hi, Mrs James, this is Dommy, my little sister." My juvenile heart started racing. "Hope you don't mind that I brought her, but it's Rosita's day off and our parents were busy."

"Not at all. But you, Kane mister, I wanted to thank you for sticking up for my baby. The only terrible part is what happened to your gorgeous face. Come on, sweetheart, let's get the cookies out. Kane, the beast is in her bedroom if you want to dare drag her out."

Gosh, Momma, how charming of you.

Now, I definitely didn't have time to reapply my make-up. I put my head back and sighed to the roof. Shrugging my shoulders, I moved to the closed door. As I opened it, I found Kane with his arm outstretched and ready to knock. He stood there frozen for a second, staring at me with his bruised right eye. The top of his nose between his eyes was also bruised.

"What?" I grumbled.

"Sorry, I think I have the wrong room; I've never seen you before. I'm Kane Stanley, and you are?" He smiled at me, holding out his hand for me to shake.

I glared down at it, and then up at him. "Nice one, smartass. You're just lucky you brought my favourite person in *your* family with you. At least now I won't be bored out of my brain." I went to push past him, but he stopped me by placing his hand on my shoulder.

"No wait, it is you, Sky. I would never mistake that potty mouth or attitude anywhere." He pulled me into a hug, his arms circling my shoulders. It shocked the hell out of me. "Thank the Lord, I thought you'd been taken over by some church-going girl, but as soon as you opened your mouth, I knew it was you."

All this because I wasn't wearing my make-up. I mock-punched him in his ribs and pushed him back. I wanted to come across as annoyed or angry, but I couldn't stop the smile forming on my face. "Keep going, jock head, and you'll be punished." I walked off.

"That could be fun," I heard behind me. He laughed as I tripped over nothing.

What was the deal with his cheeky attitude tonight? I didn't like it at all, because I liked it too much, if that made sense.

"Sky!" I heard my name screamed, and then the small blonde monster barrelled into me. Only this time, I could actually say monster because she had on a fluffy blue costume, just like she was trying to be the Cookie Monster from *Sesame Street.*

"Hey, monster, you look really cool." I smiled down at her, dislodging her arms from around my waist.

"I knew you'd like it." She looked up at me with a chocolaty mouth. "Wow, you look so pretty. But I love the make-up you wear."

"Thanks, Dom." I gave Momma a smug look and raised my eyebrows.

"Don't give me that look, girl. Besides, she's only five; she doesn't really know what she likes."

"Yes I do," Dommy pouted. "I like your cookies." She smiled.

"You're right, Momma, she doesn't know what she likes," I teased.

She snapped the tea towel at me. "Dommy, sweetheart, don't you ever grow up and give your Momma cheek."

"Did you notice one thing though, Mrs James? Dommy said that Sky looks pretty without the make-up." Kane grinned.

"Why, yes she did. So that means she thinks you look ugly with it, but is still nice enough to say she likes it."

"Stop picking on, Skylar." Dommy stomped. I loved having a five-year-old sticking up for me.

"Yeah, stop it," I mimicked.

"All right, okay." Momma laughed and then added, "Now, Dommy, let's go and find some pencils and books so you can colour while these two work before dinner."

Dommy smiled happily and started off after Momma down the hall, but quickly changed her mind, running back over to me and saying, "You know, my dad told me once that people only pick on you because they really love you."

My eyes widened. I didn't look at Kane in case he'd heard her hushed voice.

"Thanks, Dommy."

"Not that I'll pick on you, so don't worry about that. I'll just tell you I love you." She pulled my arm until I was bent over, kissed me on the cheek, and then sped out the kitchen.

"She's something, isn't she?" Kane said, and I could hear the humour and love in his voice.

"She is." I turned my back on him and opened the fridge, pretending to look for something that wasn't there. "Look, while it's quiet, I wanted to say thank you again, not that I think you should have done it. I can take care of myself. But, thank you."

"Wow, I really never expected those words to fall from your mouth. For some reason, I thought you were the type of girl who wouldn't thank a person no matter the circumstances."

I shut the fridge with a snap, turned and leaned against it, with my arms crossed over my chest and a scowl on my face.

Kane chuckled. "All right, sorry, just playing; you seem to bring it out in me." He smiled, and then his expression sobered. "I know I didn't have to, Sky, and I do know you can take care of yourself. But *I* couldn't stand by and let him speak about you like that."

My heart wanted to fly through my chest to reach out to him.

"Is that a blush? Oh, my God, I can actually see a blush on Miss Skylar's cheeks," he teased.

"Stuff it up your nose, jock boy." I glared and sat down at the table. He carefully pulled out a chair opposite me and sat. "So how's Donna after the episode?" Why did I ask that?

His shoulders hunched, his brow furrowed. "We're having a break at the moment. She didn't like the fact that I got into a fight over a girl I hardly know, and a Goth one at that."

I snorted, rolled my eyes, and opened the book in front of me. As I was trying to come across as calm on the outside, on the inside my stomach and heart played havoc.

They were having a break? What did that mean exactly?

"Sorry," I uttered.

"Honestly, I thought I'd be upset by those words. I mean, the ones where she said that things weren't working between us and that we should go our separate ways...for now. But they didn't; if anything, I felt relieved. Is that bad? I know I care for her; we've been together for what seems like forever. Still, now it's..." He looked up from his own book and blushed, then scoffed. "Listen to me. You're the last person who'd want to hear any of that stuff."

I turned away from his stare and mumbled, "I don't mind; I like the fact that you want to talk to me about things that are troubling you."

"But no advice though?"

I looked at him as he smirked.

"Sorry, I am totally the wrong girl for that crap. Josh was the longest relationship I've ever had, and look how that turned out. Besides, I don't think I should give you advice about a person I don't know, or like for that matter."

He barked out with laughter. "Point taken."

I could hear Momma and Dommy's footsteps coming back from down the hall, so I turned my attention back to the book in front of me.

"All right, we are ready. Look, sweetheart, I found your old colouring books Dommy can use, and your pencils and crayons." She laid the things on the table at the opposite end from us. Dommy was enthralled by what they'd found and sat down without a word to start looking through the colouring books. "I'll just get your dinners and then I'll be off."

"Momma, I can get them if you wanted to leave early to get one of those coffees you like."

"Someone hold me before I fall. Was that really my daughter being thoughtful?"

I rolled my eyes. I was always thoughtful; well, with Momma I was. Okay, I tried to be.

"Thank you for the thought, baby, but that's okay."

She busied herself with dinner, while Kane and I began finalising our written reports. Then we'd move on to the verbal presentation. We decided to collaborate all the information left out of our written one into a big cardboard sheet, instead of having hand cards to go off. I loved the thought because it gave me the chance to use one of those pointy stick things the teachers used to bang on their desk to get your attention and scare the crap out of you.

I'd say that by the end of the night we'd have it done, so that meant things between Kane and myself would soon come to an end.

Why did that leave me with a feeling of emptiness inside?

While Momma ran off to refresh her makeup, and Dommy had followed to watch, I tapped Kane on the arm to get his attention. Once he looked up smiling, I asked, "So, I guess if we get all this finished tonight, I won't have to suffer through more of your company and come to your house on Saturday?"

His smile faded. "I think you may be right; we should have

this done by tonight, and I'd hate to think of you suffering in my company." He went back to work.

Damn me and my big sarcastic mouth.

"Kaddy, I thought you were going to ask Sky to that thing at our house Saturday night," Dommy said, coming to sit back at the table smiling sweetly.

I turned back to Kane; he didn't look too impressed by Dommy confessing something they had obviously talked about.

"I don't think Skylar would really be interested. It's not her scene. And I'm thinking that she'll be relieved to get this assignment done with so she doesn't have to spend any more time with me." His raised his eyebrows at me, as if to say *take that.*

Dommy gasped. "Is that true, Sky? You don't like my brother?" She really sounded upset by the thought that I could have any ill feelings for Kane.

"No, it's not that. I was only joking before. I like your brother, and being around him gives me a chance to see you, and I wouldn't want it any other way."

I thought that would have felt like a lie, but I was surprised that I meant it. I liked spending time with Kane, and I really liked seeing Dommy.

"Yay, great, so you'll come Saturday night?"

"Um." I looked to Kane for any kind of help, but he didn't say anything, and just sat there smiling smugly. So I asked., "What is this thing Saturday night?"

"Just a dinner and dance thing my parents are hosting. It's going to be really boring."

"But you'll come, yeah?" Dommy asked.

"Uh—I really...is it formal?" They both nodded. Great, I'd have to wear something ordinary. Was I actually thinking about going? "Yeah, I guess." I sighed. "But what about Donna; won't she be going?"

"We're on a break, remember?"

"Right—so, you just need a fill in. I can do that. I think." That meant it wasn't a date. Kane just needed someone there to hang off his arm. That made me feel a little better. Besides, it wasn't actually him who asked; I was doing this for Dommy. Right?

"My, my, Skylar James, you actually look scared," my Momma piped in from the doorway. "Don't worry, Kane and Dommy, I will have her there on time and looking wonderful. And you can forget that God-awful makeup. Can't have you scaring off the wealthy."

Kane and Dommy laughed. I rolled my eyes and scoffed.

What was I getting myself into?

EIGHT

SKYLAR

The rest of the week flew by; it always did when you really weren't looking forward to something on the weekend. By Friday, I was ready to chew off my own arm, or knock myself out, just so I had an excuse not to attend Kane's posh affair. Unfortunately, I didn't manage to injure myself, which was why I was standing in my room late Saturday afternoon, looking at myself in my mirror and not believing what I saw. Momma and Jessie stood beside me telling me how fantastic I looked. I laughed when Jessie added at the end, "Even if it isn't Goth-looking."

Of course, I'd rang Jessie Monday night after Dommy and Kane had left. And that was after dinner, finishing our assignment, and watching one of Dommy's movies that she had brought with her called *Tangled*. It was a take-off of Rapunzel. I found myself actually liking it; I loved the horse Maximus.

Once I told Jessie where I was headed Saturday night, I had to hold the phone away as she squealed her lungs out. This ended up causing Jessie's mom to yell at her to get off the phone. So Jessie ended the conversation with, "Oh, my God, tell me everything tomorrow, and I mean *everything* that was said. Oh, babe, your first date with a rich guy." I told her it wasn't a date and that I was a 'fill in', but she didn't seem to hear that.

Kane didn't show up for school on Tuesday either. He was there for the rest of the week, only he didn't ride the bus. I heard he caught a lift from a friend. Was that because he didn't want to see Donna on the bus?

Or me? Maybe.

I was told by Jessie and Mitch that he didn't sit next to her in the other classes they had together, and at lunch, I witnessed he spent most of the time talking to his football friends. This gave Donna time, without Kane noticing, to shoot me daggers. I kind of understood that she blamed me for their break; it was because of me that Kane got into the fight in the first place.

Javis had been walking past him Wednesday morning when he overheard some of the other guys asking him what had happened to get bruised up like he had. Kane had laughed it off and told them he was saving a damsel in distress, which didn't go down well for Donna, thus why the break in their relationship. I'd been thinking that Donna hadn't told any of her friends who that said damsel was because none of them had given me crap. She was probably embarrassed about the fact that it was me— some lame Goth girl.

I needed to have a word with Kane about the damsel stuff. I was not, and never would be, a damsel. He knew this, and *I* knew that he knew that I knew—if that made sense—why had he made the whole damn damsel story up in the first place? It was obvious he didn't want anyone to know who he had saved. He'd receive too much hell from his mates because it had been me—the loser freak.

Kane and I didn't have the chance to talk during the rest of the week; of course neither of us would approach each other during school hours, and I knew he was busy afterwards with football and whatever other jock sport he played.

Another reason why I was regretting accepting the invitation

—not because he played sports after school, but because we hadn't spoken—so I was unsure if he still wanted me to be there.

This isn't me, I thought as I looked at myself for the last time. My hair was all pinned up with a few strands floating down around my face. I had on a long elegant black, backless dress— thanking God for once that my boobs weren't that big, so I didn't have to wear any of that clear tape that held boobs up.

My Momma actually went out and bought the dress for me. Yet another reason I couldn't back out, because it must have cost a bit, and when I had told her I didn't need it, she refused to take it back. Of course, then she bought me strappy black high heels to go with it. I told her it was too much just for one night, but she laughed and told me not to worry, that I'd be wearing it to my graduation party, my wedding, the birth of my first child and her funeral. I rolled my eyes, but gave her a big hug and kiss and thanked her. It was really pretty—something that I wouldn't have ever bought—meaning it was perfect for tonight.

Jessie bounced up and down beside the car. Momma was going to work late so she could drive me there...another thing to appreciate my Momma for. I found myself thinking that I didn't tell her enough, or that I didn't show her. I needed to change that.

"Oh, oh please don't forget to call me when you get home. Don't worry about my mom. I'll have the phone beside me so I'll pick it up straight away and she won't even hear it," Jesse said.

"But will you?" I knew Jessie could sleep through a chainsaw going off.

"Of course. Just call me or I will hurt you."

"Now that you have threatened my daughter, we must be off, Jessie. Are you sure you don't want a lift home?" Momma asked, leaning over me to do so.

"Thanks, Mrs J, but I'll be all right. Mitch should be here soon to pick me up."

"Now that is something you need to tell me about," I hissed and pointed in her face.

"There's nothing much to tell; it's not like we're going out or anything. We're takin' it slow—"

"What the hell for? It's not like you don't know each other already."

"Come on, girls. You've had all week to talk about this, but *now* we have to go or she'll be late and then turn into a pumpkin if she leaves past midnight tonight," Momma said.

Jessie laughed. I smiled and went to wipe my sweaty, shaking hands on my dress. Until Momma smacked my hand and passed me a handtowel that she'd had hanging over her shoulder. I thought she'd just forgotten it was there, but she must have known I'd need it.

"Have fun, Princess, and talk to ya later." Jessie winked and then waved once we started to drive off.

❦

"Now don't worry, Skylar. You walk in there with your head held high, like you belong. Remember, you are there for Kane and Dommy; they need and want you there and that's all that matters. And please make sure you have fun. I'll see you in the morning, sweetheart. Love you, baby." She gave me a kiss on the cheek, leaned over me to open the door, and shoved me out. She didn't want to drive me up to the house because of the way our car looked; it was only a little run-down with a bit of rust. But when I really looked at all the cars driving up the long driveway, I understood—most of them were limousines.

Everything in me was saying to run, get back home, that I didn't need to do this.

Yeah, I felt really out of my comfort zone. Still, I took a deep breath, lifted my dress up a little, and started forward.

Once at the door, a large body builder guy with a deep gravelly voice barked, "Name?"

"Uh—Skylar James."

He looked down his list, and for a moment there, I thought Kane had forgotten to put my damn name down on a list I didn't even know I needed to be on. I mean, come on, we weren't going into an exclusive nightclub or anything.

In the end, he gave me a small nod for me to enter. I gulped and walked through. The house looked exactly the same; the only difference was there were a lot of older people dressed in their best clothing, walking around with their noses up to the ceiling.

Nearing the stairs, I heard my name being bellowed, "Sky!" In the next second, I was nearly knocked to the ground. I looked down to find Dommy hugging me close. She looked up and smiled. "You look really beautiful."

"Thanks, kiddo. You brush up well too." And she did; she looked like a little princess would, in a long, pink, frilly dress, topped off with a tiara. "Where's your pain-in-the-butt brother?" He was the one who got me into this mess; the least he could do was be here.

"I heard that." I turned to find Kane standing there smiling. He was dressed in a black tuxedo. As he took my outfit in from head to toe with an appreciative gleam in his eyes, I gazed over him.

"Penguin suit? Wow." He did actually look really double damn fine. Fine enough to get my heart rate up.

He smirked. "Tell me about it; this is another reason why we both hate these types of gigs. Alas, we have to put up with it for our parents."

"And you dragged me into one." I glared.

"Thanks to Dommy." He grinned, crossing his arms over his chest, looking very pleased with himself.

What? No way could a five-year-old play me. I looked down to question said little demon-angel, but she was nowhere to be seen.

"Do you mean to tell me that I've been played by a five-year-old to get me here?" I said through clenched teeth.

"She is a great actress." He took a step forward and placed his arms down to his sides. "Come on, Skylar, I knew you wouldn't come if I had just asked. So I asked for Dommy's help. She was more than willing; she loves having you around. And...I thought...look, I knew it wouldn't be so boring if I had you here."

What the hell? Was he actually blushing? Yes, there it was. Damn, how could I stay mad at that?

"Damn you and your evil sidekick." I glared. But not being able to hide my twitching mouth.

"Are you cranky now Sky?" Dommy asked from a few feet away. You would think that I wouldn't be able to hear her from the house being so full with people, but those said people were in their own private hushed conversations. Even the soft classical music being played in the background didn't stop the monster from being heard.

"No." I smiled. "But I think I'm going to have to keep a close eye on you from now on though."

"So you're not mad?"

"No, how could I stay mad at you? Now your brother is another matter," I said, glancing at Kane, who gave me an innocent face.

"Great, as long as you're not mad at me." Dommy grinned.

"Thanks, squirt." Kane chuckled. "Now, let's go dance."

"What? Wait, no one said anything about dancing." New nerves kicked in.

"Don't worry, Sky. I'll help you," Dommy said, taking my hand in hers and leading me into a room opposite their library, which turned out to be a large hall. At least a room like that came in handy for those types of events. Though, I could never see myself wanting a house with a room like that in it. I just knew that when it wasn't being used, it would feel—well, empty and cold.

Still, it took my breath away. People danced on the dance floor; there were tables to the far right side full of food, and to the other end was the band playing their music. I stifled my laugh because they looked really bored with the music they were playing. Straight across were tables and chairs for people to sit at when eating.

It only took me a couple of seconds to take all that in. The next hour or so I spent dancing with Kane and Dommy.

If only my Momma could've seen me. She wouldn't believe it, and even though I was the one dancing around holding onto a hand of Kane's and a small hand of Dommy's, I couldn't comprehend how much fun I was having. Dommy loved to dance, and even though it was light classical music being played, she threw in some rock, ballet, and hip-hop dance moves. I had never laughed so much.

Of course, we received a few odd looks from people, but if Kane didn't care, then I didn't let it get to me. I already thought my heart was beating enough from all the dancing, but when Dommy said that she was going to get a drink and Kane took me into his arms for a slow dance, I thought I was going to have a heart attack.

He pulled me close, one hand still in mine and the other went to my waist. Just that one touch of his fingers on my bare back sent shivers throughout my body. I clamped my mouth closed to hold in my moan.

"Are you cold?" Kane whispered. He was so close to my ear that I could feel his warm breath on my neck.

Being so close only means he won't have to speak so loud.

I gulped, which I think he heard because the next second, he chuckled.

"No—I, um, I'm fine," I stuttered like a fool.

"You, um, look really beautiful tonight," Kane uttered into my ear. I wanted to move back to look into his eyes, but I was afraid of what I would find in them. Instead, I nodded into his shoulder.

He moved me around the dance floor like a pro. This guy had to have had dance lessons, or he was just one of those people who had natural rhythm. Unlike myself, who was lucky that Kane was great at leading.

I was enjoying his touch too much; I needed some air and soon. Thankfully, Dommy gave me the chance to make a break.

"I think someone is ready for bed," I said to Kane, gesturing with my head to look to the left where Dommy sat on a chair, which she was nearly falling off with her eyes half-closed.

Kane laughed. "I think you may be right. I'll go and get Rosita; she's always in the kitchen on these kind of nights."

He went to walk off, but I grabbed his sleeve quickly. "No, do you mind if I do it?"

"Really?" He seemed surprised.

"Yeah." I nodded. He took hold of my hand and led me over to Dommy. She didn't even take any notice of us standing in front of her.

I went to pick her up until I felt movement to the side of me. I stood up straight and turned around. Standing there were the older versions of Kane and Dommy.

"Kane, who do we have here?" Mrs Stanley asked.

"This is a friend of mine from school, Skylar James."

"Oh, you're the one who is doing the history paper with our son." Mr Stanley smiled.

"Yes, sir. It's so nice to meet you both, and thank you for having me in your beautiful home." Momma did actually teach me manners.

"Thank you, dear," Mrs. Stanley said, looking anywhere but at me. "Kane, where is your girlfriend, Donna tonight?"

Now that was a slap in the face if I ever heard one before. I could feel Kane stiffen beside me.

"Mommy, I want to go to bed." Saved once again by Dommy.

"All right, sweetheart, I'll call Rosita."

"It's fine, Mom. I was going to take her."

Mrs Stanley rolled her eyes and sighed. "Fine, if that is what you want to do. But when you come back down, Kane, I wish for you to mingle."

Oh, oh, who was the boss in the house? Why, it was Evil Mom.

It was pretty obvious that I would not be welcomed back again.

"Sure, Mom." Kane frowned. He scooped up Dommy in his arms, and she held on around his neck as he strode off. I quickly followed behind.

"Sorry about that," Kane uttered once we got Dommy changed and into bed. I pulled the blankets up over her as she snuggled down tighter.

"Don't worry about it," I whispered. I bent over and gave Dommy a quick kiss on the cheek; she stirred and looked up with tired eyes, saying, "Sky, I had so much fun tonight; thank you for coming. Pleeeease say you'll be back."

I smiled down at her. "Of course, hon, nothing can keep me away from another *Ruby Gloom* fan. Now, go to sleep."

"Night, Kane."

"Night, squirt."

We left the room, and Kane silently closed the door behind us while I leaned against the wall. Kane took my hand and led me back down the stairs. I was reluctant to go back into the hall. I grinned when he headed towards the library. He opened the door, and closed it once we were inside; the thick door blocked out most of the sound. I was starting to feel tired myself; dancing sure did take a lot out of you.

Would Kane be able to hear my heart beating wildly from where he stood near the door? I kept walking over to the window to look out at the night's sky. The stars were shining brightly; it didn't seem windy out there, and I hoped it would stay like that because I didn't bring a jacket to wear home. Momma had given me some money for a taxi home that I stuffed in my sweaty shoe.

Um, gross. Sorry, taxi driver, whoever you would be.

I turned to see what Kane was doing, and jumped when I found him right behind me. Kane stepped closer as a small smile played at the corner of his lips. We both stared at each other. Then he reached out with one hand to tuck a loose strand of hair behind my ear. His touch was warm and inviting, causing me to close my eyes and enjoy the feel of it.

"This is the only reason I had second thoughts of asking you here," he whispered.

I opened my eyes, looking at him sceptically. He laughed, but then stopped when he ran his hand from my face down to cup the back of my neck. He continued, "Whenever I'm around you, Skylar James, I can't think straight and I always want to touch you."

Again, I gulped, and then cleared my throat to say, "Well, I think it could be a bad idea bringing me into a room alone."

He chuckled, and then sobered to ask, "Do you want me to step back?"

"I–uh…"

A knock at the door saved me from answering. Kane walked over to answer it, and I decided to follow him. I think it would have been a great idea if we left the room, because if we stayed there alone and he asked me that question again, I wouldn't be able to say yes.

Kane opened the door and Rosita quickly squeezed her way in, pushing Kane back in the process. She didn't seem surprised to see me in here with him; she gave me a wave and a smiled, then said to Kane with a disappointed look, "Miss Donna is here looking for you."

My heart dropped to my feet. I was sure Kane turned pale. Honestly, I felt for him; he nearly made a mistake with me and it was like getting a cold splash of water in the face to find out his girlfriend—even though they were on a break—was, in fact, here to see him. Maybe even to reconcile things between them.

I gripped my stomach. I felt sick.

Next, there was another knock at the door, which made us all jump, and then Donna called out for Kane. Rosita opened the door and went out; Kane followed her, mouthing to me that he wouldn't be long.

Yeah, right.

I went over to the wall for some help in supporting myself. Okay, to be honest, I got closer to see if I could hear the conversation, which I could.

"Donna, what are you doing here?" Kane asked.

"Your mother called and said that she thought I should come, and it wasn't the same without me being here on your arm."

"Of course she did." Kane sighed loudly.

"Kane, look, I really am sorry for the way I acted. If I thought it would have caused you to tell me we needed a break, then I wouldn't have said what I did."

Say what now? Kane was the one who asked for the break? What had Donna said for him to do that?

I let my own thoughts die when I heard Donna speak again, "I will never act that way again; just please say that it was all silly. I promise I *will* make it up to you."

I just knew she was rubbing herself up against him, but unfortunately, I had no right to run out there and slam her face into the ground. Which was what I really wanted to do.

"No more waiting, baby. Your mom gave her permission for me to spend the night…in your room, honey," she cooed.

It fell silent out there. Oh God, were they kissing while I was standing just a few feet away? Or worse, was he actually going to say, 'Yahoo, I'll race you upstairs,' and forget that I was even in the house?

"Rosita, what is it?" Kane asked.

"Nothing, Mr Kane. Excuse me for a second." The door to the library opened and Rosita came in.

"Donna, I…"

I didn't hear the rest, what caught my undivided attention

was the look on Rosita's face; she looked upset and concerned. She closed the door with one hand and had a phone in the other.

"Rosita, what is it?" I asked panicked, my hand going to my throat.

"It is for you, Senorita." She held out the phone. I took it with a shaking hand and held it up to my ear. Rosita stepped closer, her arm going around my waist.

"Hello?"

"Oh, Sky, honey." I recognized the voice straight away. It was Barbra Keating, my Momma's best friend from her work.

Oh no, this couldn't be good if she was ringing me here.

"It's your Momma, honey. There was a robbery at the store. Oh, honey, he—the man had a gun…"

Thankfully, Rosita was there, or else I would have fallen to the floor. "No, no, no. Not Momma, please…"

"Sky, hon, listen. She's been shot; she's at the hospital. I'm here now, but—hon, I don't know… she's being operated on now. Come here, honey; she'll want to see you when she gets out."

If she gets out. No! I will not think like that.

"I'll be there soon."

"Good girl; the Base Hospital. I'll see you soon."

I passed the phone to Rosita's waiting hand. Had I even hung it up? I didn't know.

Damn it to hell. Oh shit, my Momma had been shot.

How could this happen?

Not to her. She didn't need this. Damn it, she had better pull through.

I wanted to cry. I wanted to sink to the ground and sob. But that would get me nowhere, and when I couldn't cry, I got angry. That was better than breaking down.

"I have to go," I uttered, my fist clenched at my sides.

"Yes, go, child. I am sorry."

I nodded. Without thinking, I opened the door, picked up

the bottom of my dress so I wouldn't trip over, and ran. I kept running, ignoring Donna yelling, "What is she doing here?" Ignoring Kane asking me, "Skylar, what's wrong?"

What was wrong?

A million things.

I didn't stop, even when I heard the words that nearly broke me again from Rosita, "Her Momma has been shot while working." And Kane's audible answer of, "Shit."

No, I kept moving out the front door, out into the cold night air.

PART TWO

NINE

ALEXANDRA

On a sigh, I wondered what was going to be in store for me today at Rushton High School.

Probably something disastrous, like the last couple of days, since I was klutzy enough to trip over my own two feet and land on the floor at the feet of Miss Cummins and Mr Haydn. I'd had everyone's attention and my usual invisible geekiness was no longer working. All I heard every day since then was that I was falling for Mr Haydn, or that I was trying to look up Miss Cummins's skirt.

Of course, I was doing neither. What I had actually been doing was trying to make enough room in the hallway for Tristan Davis and his crew to walk past. It was their teasing of others in the first place I wanted to stay away from. They were the worst, especially Tom Sinker, Hunter Gresham, and Aaron Kellie; the three of them together were trouble. Now that I no longer blended into the background after that one hiccup, they tried to flirt with me—only not in a good way. They probably thought I loved the attention they gave me. But I didn't; I loathed it. Who wouldn't?

Who would want to walk into a room or pass by them while getting their bottoms pinched or slapped, or something thrown at them, like food or sports equipment? Or being pulled onto their laps as everyone laughed along with them. I tried to look to Tristan for any kind of help. I found he was the one who seemed to be able to control them, because when he spoke, they listened. But every time I did, he'd turn his scowling face away.

My dad had always told me to ignore stupid teenaged boys. So I did. I no longer flinched when I felt a pinch or when something was thrown my way. I took it all, and hoped that one day they'd give up.

I didn't have enough guts to stand up to them. I wished I did. All I wanted to do was go to school, learn, graduate, and move on to university without too many emotional scars to bring me down.

Letting out another sigh, I pushed my glasses back up my nose and opened the front door to my school. So far so good, no sign of any of them.

"Hi, Alex."

I jumped high and grabbed at my chest when Corbet appeared out of nowhere. Corbet was like me in many ways. We loved to learn. We loved to eat Italian food, listened to eighties music, and studied. He was a great friend to have and I'd been lucky enough to have him since kindergarten. Just like Sarah, who was walking towards us—not the kindergarten part, but being a great friend. Sarah moved here two years ago, and since then, we'd been stuck like glue. Not that anyone could understand it—we were two totally different people.

"Jeez, Corbet, you gave me a heart-attack," I complained.

"I told him not to do it." Sarah smiled and gave me a quick hug.

Sometimes, I wondered why Sarah hung out with us. I mean, yes, she liked the things we did, but where Corbet and I both looked the geek part, she didn't. I had dark, ocean-blue eyes. I was small and stubby, and had long, boring brown hair that was always being pushed behind my ears. Corbet was cute in his own way. He was a few inches taller than me, and skinny, with light brown hair and eyes. He also wore glasses, like me. As for Sarah, she was tall, slim, but not rake skinny, and beautiful with her long, dark red hair and light emerald eyes. She was also lucky enough to be so good-looking that no one seemed to bother her.

"Sorry, Alex. I really should have thought it through," Corbet said with sympathy in his eyes. He knew who I thought it was. Unfortunately, he got just as much unwanted attention from the 'three stooges' as I did.

"It's all right." I started to walk with them beside me. We had the same Social Studies class to get to, and the bell was going to ring any second.

"How was your weekend, girls?" Corbet asked as we reached the door in time. The bell sounded when we walked in.

"Good, we watched the two *Bridget Jones* movies; you should have come," Sarah said. Every weekend we did the same thing: sleep over at my house, rent movies, and pig out on takeaway and junk food. My dad didn't mind; he was usually working on some court case anyway. He liked that I had the company on weekends when he was too busy. Made him feel less guilty. Not that he should, we'd been through enough after my mom passed away from cancer a year-and-a-half ago. Dad threw himself into work, and I threw myself more into studies and my new job at the local library.

"You know I would have, but I had that thing with the family." Corbet sighed, sitting in his seat in front of our table and next to Laura Jennings, the class gossip and top cheerleader. He wouldn't usually sit next to her, but she was moved tables when she and her best friend Brittany wouldn't stop texting and talking.

Corbet was talking about his family's reunion picnic they had every year. He hated them, but was made to go by his parents, or else he would have spent the night with us as well. Another thing my dad didn't mind; he trusted me.

The teacher walked in and started speaking, so the class

quieted at once. Everyone knew not to face the wrath of Mr Kenneth; he was one hard teacher to get on his good side with. It took Laura a few classes to figure that out, and only when she was moved to sit with Corbet did she finally get it.

He wasn't a bad teacher; I got along with him fine, but Sarah had said that was because I had good grades all the time. I felt Sarah nudge my arm with her elbow; once she got my attention, she slid a piece of paper towards me.

He likes you.

I looked at her puzzled and scribbled back. *Who???*

She rolled her eyes and wrote, *Corbet!!!*

I stifled a laugh and shook my head, while winding my finger around my ear to signal she was crazy.

Fine, deny it, but I know it's true. By the way... I kissed someone.

I couldn't stop the gasp, thankfully no one—especially the teacher—heard.

Who??? When??? Where???

She giggled, wrote something, and then slid the piece of paper back.

Opening it, I read:

Sunday night! My parents made me go to the grocery store; he was there. We started talking. I found I liked him, and kissed him before I left.

I raised my eyebrows at her. She didn't answer the one question I wanted the most, which didn't sit well with me, so I wrote back.

WHO???

She looked reluctant to tell me, but finally started writing and passed it back slowly.

Please don't be mad...Tristan Davis.

My heart started racing. Oh God, why would she have done that? He was their ringleader, and she knew how much I despised them.

Hang on a minute...what was that other thing I was feeling

in the pit of my stomach, nauseous? Hate? Regret? Enmity? Jealousy?

Sarah grabbed another piece of paper and quickly wrote. *Please, please don't hate me.*

I don't. I could never! But what does this mean? I wrote.

She shrugged and scribbled down, *I don't know, but I think I like him, and he's a great kisser!!*

I nodded at her, not knowing what to write back. I was grateful when she turned her attention back to what the teacher was saying. I wish I could have as well, but my mind wouldn't allow it.

I shouldn't really think too much about it; Sarah liked a different guy each week. It wouldn't last. And why was I *hoping* that it wouldn't?

I didn't know Tristan at all; we'd never spoken and he was definitely not my type. All right, so he may be good looking in a bad-boy way, with his shoulder-length black hair and dark brown eyes. He was very tall and broad in a giant's kind of way. Way too tall for my liking.

Maybe what I was feeling had something to do with the slight envy I had for Sarah. She was beautiful and it seemed she could have any guy she liked. Where I'd never been on a date and had kissed only one guy who dribbled everywhere. No one of the opposite sex had any feeling for me whatsoever.

Yes, Sarah did say something about Corbet liking me, but I couldn't see it. We were friends and that was all we would ever be. Besides, if he did, which I wasn't saying he did, I couldn't like him like that, and I knew I never would.

The bell rang, telling me it was time to move to my next class: Maths.

"We'll talk later, okay?" Sarah whispered. I nodded before she left the room with Corbet, who gave me a quick wave walking out the door. They both had English together next period, so that left me stuck in Maths all alone with Tristan and his idiots. I only had to go next door for it.

Holding my breath, I walked through the door and sighed in relief seeing that they hadn't arrived yet. I shouldn't have gotten too excited though; before I made it to me desk in the middle of the class, I felt a hard smack on my rear. That time it made me jump; I looked over my shoulder to see Aaron standing there grinning. I wanted to rub where he'd hit because it was still stinging, but I knew that would only make things worse. So I quickly sat down, saying nothing.

"Come on, doll, you know you liked it. When are you going to just come out with it and tell me how much you want my body?" He laughed and others followed suit. I think they did it mainly to keep him happy and to hide the fact they were happy he wasn't doing it to any of them.

"How do you know she doesn't want *my* body?" Tom added as he sat in his seat in the back next to Aaron. I didn't say anything, but watched out the corner of my eye as Tristan and Hunter walked in and also sat in the back.

"What's going on, chaps?" Hunter asked.

"Nothing much, just waiting for Alex there to tell us which one she has the hots for," Aaron supplied.

"Maybe she likes us all...could make it fun." Hunter laughed. They then started talking about what position they'd like to have me in. I couldn't stop the blush from rising.

"Oh, look, just us talking about it has her hot and ready." Tom snickered.

Thankfully, the teacher, Mrs Hemingway, walked in and started the class. It didn't take long to tune out whatever else they were saying and concentrate on cosine and tangent ratio. I loved Maths; it was my best subject. Even though I still got good grades for all my subjects, Maths was the one I enjoyed the most.

Only, it was always too soon when it finished. The bell rang for lunch; I quickly packed up my things, and started to head out before the idiots had left their seats.

"Miss Harmony, I would like to have a word with you please."

I hunched my shoulders and turned back around to the teacher. I walked over to her desk before the guys came my way; they wouldn't risk doing or saying anything in front of the teacher. It was only when the class had emptied that I noticed Tristan still in the room in his seat in the back.

"Tristan, come up here," Mrs. Hemingway ordered. She had that voice where you knew to do as she said or else you'd suffer the consequences. She was a tough teacher like Mr Kenneth, who stuck strictly to the rules. She had been teaching here a long time and was now in her mid-sixties, with long grey hair that was always in a ponytail, and dark blue eyes.

"Alex," she said, bringing my attention back to her. "I was speaking to Tristan here last Friday, informing him that if he didn't pull up his grade that he will be failing this class. We both don't want that to happen, so I suggested that he find a study partner, someone who has all of the knowledge of what needs to be learned. I think that someone is you."

I couldn't help it; I gaped. Was she serious? Me, help Tristan with Maths? Me, in a room alone with Tristan? Me?

"I don't want her," Tristan said quietly. His answer didn't surprise me; who would want me?

"You do not get a choice on who is helping you, Tristan. Just be grateful for that said help."

"I can't," I said and flinched away from Tristan.

"Why not?" the teacher asked.

Yes, why not, Alex? Think, damn it, think. This was where my brain should be supplying me with a suitable answer. Instead, I got nothing.

"I—ah." I shrugged. *Great one, Alex, make the guy hate me even more by rejecting him without an answer.*

"Alex, unless you can come up with a good explanation, I see no way around this. You are the best candidate for teaching Tristan." She waited for me to say something, but still, I had nothing. My brain had failed me for the first time.

"Well, let's see; I think getting together three times a week should be sufficient..."

"I can't do three; I still have to work, and that's Monday, Tuesday, Wednesday and Thursday nights," Tristan said.

"All right, two then. Friday nights and Saturday. Let's say at the local library."

"I work there Friday afternoons and Saturdays," I said. Mrs Hemingway sunk in her seat and sighed in defeat. This was looking promising; our schedules didn't correspond, so I wouldn't be able to help him.

"I can come by after you finish on both days." Tristan sneered.

On that, Mrs Hemingway perked back up and smiled. My stomach dropped; damn it again, why couldn't he have just kept his mouth shut.

"Very good then. Alex, what time do you finish on both days?"

I rolled my eyes. "Seven Fridays and twelve Saturdays."

"Great, that gives you two hours Friday night before the library closes, and half the day Saturday."

"I do have a life, you know; I'm not spending all my Saturday in the freaking library," Tristan complained.

"Doesn't matter. I'm sure the two of you will work out how long you'll need to study for. Now, you both best be off or you'll miss lunch." With that, she grabbed her things and walked out of the classroom.

I was not going to be standing there alone with Tristan, so I quickly followed her out. Though, Tristan was still fast enough to catch me on the way to the cafeteria and growled in a whisper, "You tell no one you're helping me."

Like I would want anyone to know. That was what I wanted to say; instead, I nodded my head, and he kept walking.

I went through the doors to the crowded, smelly, and noisy

lunchroom. Right then, I didn't feel like eating, so I went to the table that was already occupied by Sarah. I looked over to the line at the counter and found Corbet there waiting to be served, no doubt for his second helping; he loved his food.

"Hi." I smiled.

Sarah looked up from her tray and smiled back. "Oh hey, I didn't think you were talking to me."

"Why would I do that?" I asked while getting an apple from my bag.

"About, you know, the whole Tristan thing. I know you hate him and his friends, and I totally understand why. But I think Tristan is different from those other wankers."

By the way he just growled at me, I doubted it. Still, I answered with, "Yeah, you might be right. So it wasn't a one off thing?"

"I don't know; I hope not. He's such a great kisser. I haven't seen him today though; was he in Maths?"

Yeah, and I have to help him study in private later. Alone. My body shuddered; was I scared? Probably.

"Yes. He was there."

Her eyes brightened. "Good, I hope I see him later. See if I can get a vibe whether he wants to continue on from last night or forget about it."

I hope he forgets about it.

What? Where did that come from? I know; it was because I didn't want to see Sarah get hurt, and Tristan was more than capable of doing just that.

"What are you cooking for tea tonight?" Sarah asked.

"Trying to see if it's going to be better than what you'll be getting?" I smirked. She was always doing that. I cooked most weeknights. Dad always got home late, so I found it easier instead of waiting for him to cook—which always seemed to get burnt. So I took over the cooking, and the washing, and the cleaning. He had enough on his plate with work, and that was the last thing he needed to come home to do. So Sarah, who had always liked my cooking, usually ended up at my house for tea. It sure beat eating alone, and it wasn't like her parents would care. Ever since my mom passed away, they'd been very supportive, letting Sarah come over all the time to keep me company. Besides, they thought I was a good influence on her.

For once, I was grateful for the chores. I needed to keep my mind extra busy, because if it wasn't, I knew I'd start thinking of the looming Friday and Saturday with Tristan.

Would he even listen to me? There was a chance he wouldn't turn up. I could just hope he wouldn't start tormenting me for the answers like his mates did.

For the first time in my life, I was not looking forward to going to work Friday.

TEN

ALEXANDRA

Friday arrived too quickly.

I usually looked forward to going to work, but this afternoon, I wasn't and it all had to do with Tristan, who would be turning up any minute. I felt nauseated and found I was having problems all afternoon, putting books away in the wrong places, spelling people's names incorrectly. Even with the simplest names like Smith, I typed into the computer Sinth, which caused the customer to look at me strangely. I even had Mrs Doherty, my supervisor, asking me what the matter was, because I had never behaved like that before. I told her I wasn't feeling well, and that I was still in for a long night because I had to tutor someone after my shift had finished. She smiled and asked if it was a boy. I, of course, blushed and said yes, and then she said "Ah-huh," as though that explained everything, and then walked off. But the thing was it *didn't* explain everything; she probably thought I had some silly little crush on Tristan, and it would never have crossed her mind that he was the ringleader of a bunch of idiots that caused me trouble every day at school.

I couldn't keep my mind from picturing how the tutoring episode would go, or if he'd even show. If he did, would he ignore me and my help, like he ignored his idiots when they were hassling me? Only time would tell, and I wished time would just stop so I didn't really have to find out.

Anxiety crept over me. I glanced up to the clock on the wall opposite our desk to see that my shift had finished. I grumbled to myself, collected my things, said a 'see you later' to Mrs Doherty, and then walked over to a table in the far corner behind some tall bookstands.

Okay, so for a second it may have crossed my mind that he wouldn't be able to find me.

I waited there for ten minutes on my own, telling myself that if he did not show up in the next five minutes I would leave. I opened the book, "Demon Princess" that I had borrowed before my shift started and began to read. People—mainly Sarah—asked why I read those types of supernatural books when my smart brain could handle so much more. That was when I told her and anyone else who asked that maybe my brain enjoyed the break by totally losing myself in a different kind of story. I did love reading any kind of supernatural romance novels; they took me to another place. I didn't understand when people said they hated to read. Then I figured it was only because they didn't have the imagination. When the story unfolds itself in our minds, it was very gratifying and could, if I let it, entertain me for hours. In a way, everything around me vanished—for instance, when someone walked up to the table I was still sitting at and stood there for God knows how long until I felt his presence.

I looked up from the book to see Tristan staring down at me with a solemn look upon his face.

"You're late," I snapped, then gasped and placed my hand over my mouth. Did I really just speak to him like that? "Sorry," I uttered.

He rolled his eyes and sat down. "Yeah, I had to do some stuff before coming here. Do you still want to do this today, or just make it tomorrow where I should be on time?"

Was he trying to get out of this already? Was it that hard to be around me? What had kept him so busy in the first place to make him late? And why was I caring?

"No, no. I am sure we can make a start on it tonight." I looked at my phone. I had been reading for half an hour. If that was so, then why did he ever bother coming?

"I mean, if that's all right with you?" I quickly added.

"Whatever." He shrugged and sunk lower in the seat. Seeing he had brought nothing to work with, I pulled out the spare empty notebook that I'd had at home and some pencils. I liked to come prepared for these situations, and something told me that I would have needed them when Tristan was concerned.

I started writing things down. "All right, we'll start with Tangent Ratio. Do you understand the solution?"

He sighed, leaned forward, took the pencil out of my hand, and began writing something down as he said, "Tangent equals opposite side over the adjacent side, and that's all I *do* know." He threw the pencil down and sat back.

"That's all right; it's a start." I smiled. He glared at my encouragement, so I quickly continued. "If you just look at how I work it out. it may help."

In the next half-hour, I tried to get something to sink into Tristan's brain. I spent most of the time talking, which I expected when teaching someone something. What I didn't expect was that Tristan actually listened. He didn't interrupt. He didn't say anything for me to think that I wasn't helping, or that I was silly in how I wanted to approach the subject with him. And for that I was grateful. Although, sometimes it was hard to concentrate, and my own mind would blank when he would stare at me with intense eyes, or he'd turn his head to the side a little when trying to understand what I was saying. At least that was when I knew to repeat it and he'd straighten his head and nod at me. I felt that I liked that; I liked helping someone understand something I knew, and when he finally started making progress, it warmed me on the inside thinking that I'd helped him do that.

"By George, I think you have it." I beamed.

He looked at me confused. "What?"

A blush rose and I looked away to pack the things in my bag. "Sorry, just something my mom used to say."

"Okay." He nodded. "So I'll meet you here tomorrow at twelve?"

"Yes. Oh, but what happens if something comes up? Or you're running late? I'd like to know so I don't wait all day. So, um—if I give you my number you could text me." I hope he didn't think that I was trying to push myself at him.

He raised his eyebrows. "All right, what is it?" He grabbed his phone out of his hooded jumper. I rattled off my number as he typed it in. "It's Alex, right?" he asked.

Really? He wasn't sure of my name? I felt the urge to roll my eyes, but I contained it. Instead, an inconvenient blush rose again. Not because I was embarrassed, but I was annoyed that he thought he had my name wrong. Luckily for him, he didn't or I would have...oh, who was I trying to trick? I wouldn't have done or said anything.

Instead, I sighed and said, "Yes."

"Do you want mine in case you're late or something?" This time he gave me a small smirk.

"No. Thank you. I work here, remember? So I won't be late."

He seemed puzzled by my answer. Was it because I wouldn't be one of those millions of girls who would fall at his strong feet wanting the phone number of one of the most sexy, rough, tall, strongly built, intriguing guys around.

That was not me.

"You don't like me, do you?" he asked.

I paused what I was doing and looked at him. "I don't know you. Anyway, would you really care if I didn't?"

He shrugged and stood. "I guess not. See you tomorrow, *Alex,*" he said and left.

There was no thank you for your help, or anything. Why did that not surprise me?

I shook my head and strapped my pack up so none of the many books inside fell out. I threw it over my shoulder and walked out of the library, saying my final goodbye to Mrs Doherty on the way. I stood just outside the entrance as the cool night air hit me. I knew I should have grabbed an extra jacket and my gloves. I looked up to the clear night sky, while wishing the breeze away. Instead of getting what I asked for, another gust of wind blew, nearly pulling me over, the weight of my bag not helping. I stumbled back until something solid caught me.

I looked around to thank whoever it was now helping me straighten up with their hand under my arm, and found Tristan standing there, a tight expression across his face. Where had he come from?

"You should be more careful. Don't you have another jacket or something? It's freezing out here."

I stood stunned for a second, then remembered he'd asked me something, so I quickly replied, "As you can see, I don't have a jacket or else I would be wearing it." Did that sound sarcastic? That sounded rude, didn't it? I looked away from him, down to my feet. "Sorry. Thanks for the help though." I went to walk off, realising then that he still had a hold of my arms. His touch firm, but warm. Welcoming?

What?

He removed his hands quickly and shrugged out of his jacket that I hadn't seen him wearing before. He went to place it around my shoulders, but I stepped back and placed my hand on his strong arm.

"No, you have it; it's yours and I don't live that far from here." Why was he being nice to me? Was it because of my helping in Maths?

"Your tiny body will need it more than me," he said with an eye roll. "Or is it because it's mine? You hate the thought of having something of mine touch you?" He glared.

"Don't be ridiculous...and tiny body? That's just mean." I glared back and snatched his jacket out of his hands, thrusting my arms into the too-long sleeves. I quickly pushed them up and looked back up to Tristan's amused face. I sighed. "Sorry, I didn't mean that *you're* ridiculous, just what you said..."

"Do you always apologise when you stick up for yourself?"

I thought about it for a second. Though I already knew that was exactly what I did. "Yes."

"You shouldn't."

I knew that, but when you did something for so long, it was hard to stop.

"That's what Sarah's always telling me."

Sarah...just thinking about her reminded me that Tristan had only just last night kissed her and that she wanted more of it. "You know Sarah, right?"

He shook his head. "No. Should I?"

I felt offended on Sarah's behalf. Did he go around kissing so many girls that he forgot which ones he had?

"Sarah, tall, red hair, goes to our school?" He kept shaking his head. I growled and stomped my foot. "You kissed her last night at the grocery store. Ring any bells now? Or is she just one of many that you kissed last night?" I gasped, my hand flying to my mouth. I shouldn't have said that. "Sorry," I uttered.

He rolled his eyes. I thought he'd be peeved with what I just said, but he was smiling.

"Now I know who you're talking about. I was confused. Not because of all the *many* I apparently kiss, but because she didn't mention her name. We were talking, and then she said she had to go, and then kissed *me*. I am not one to push someone away who wants just a mere kiss."

Really? She kissed him? A mere kiss? What was that supposed to mean? Didn't kissing someone mean something to him? I knew it would me, if anyone kissed me.

And why was I pleased that he didn't remember her?

"It doesn't matter; it's none of my business. Only that..."

Was I really going to say this? "I think she likes you and…maybe wants to see you again." *Yes, I did just say that.*

"Really? Well, I guess we'll see what happens." He smirked.

"Hey, that you, Tristan?" Someone yelled behind him. Tristan stiffened. I went to glance around him to see who it was, but he gripped my shoulders and held me in place.

"You need to go," he said through clenched teeth.

"Yo, Tristan."

Then I recognized the voice; it was Aaron, and when there was one idiot, the others wouldn't be far behind.

It all dawned on me then. Tristan didn't want them to see me with him. Questions would be asked, ones that he wouldn't want answered. Why would the rebel in school want to be associated with the dork? I got it; I did. Still, it did hurt.

I didn't bother saying anything; I turned and walked quickly around the side of the library, knowing that Tristan's solid form would hide my *tiny* body from being seen. Once there, I stopped and listened.

"Hey, man, what the hell are you doing here?" Aaron asked.

"Nothing much, hassling the workers. Been searchin' for you and the others. Speaking of which, where are they?"

"Around the corner at Joe's Pool Hall. I stepped out for a breather with a pretty brunette, then she friggin' left me; that's when I spotted you."

"All right, let's go have some fun then," Tristan said, sounding bored.

"Now you're talking."

I waited until I could no longer hear their retreating footsteps and walked out from around the corner. What I should have done was walk into Joe's with my head held high and thrown his stupid jacket at his face. Of course, I didn't. Instead, I pulled his jacket tighter around me, taking in the scent of Tristan that was left behind. He smelled wonderful.

I couldn't be upset with him, and I shouldn't care about what just took place. I thought we were getting along fine. It went to show you how different people could be when they didn't hang around with their usual crowd. Question was: which was the real Tristan?

Didn't matter. All I had to do was help him get his grade up in Maths, which I was sure I'd be able to. Then we could go back to the way things were. I'd be that invisible girl I always was to him, and he'd be the ringleader of the idiots.

Really, that hadn't changed for him.

ELEVEN

ALEXANDRA

Sleep was hard to come Friday night.

I was still awake at two in the morning when Dad came home. At least he sounded like he was in a happy mood, whistling away. That meant he must have won the case he'd been working on. I wanted to get up and talk to him; it seemed we hardly got to see each other, but I didn't. My bed was too warm and the house was too cold. The last thing I remembered before finally falling asleep was dad opening my door to check I was where I was supposed to be.

I woke to my alarm ringing at nine. Usually, I'd be up and awake by seven, but the lack of sleep had me sleeping late. Actually, I wanted to roll back over and go back to sleep, but I was never one to call in a sick day when I wasn't really ill. Especially when it was my own silly fault for being awake so late in the first place. I couldn't stop my brain from thinking...about Tristan. I kept looking at his coat hanging over my chair at my desk; his scent from it was overpowering enough that I could smell it from across the room as I laid in my bed.

Why would he do something nice like that, and then have me hide away when one of his idiot mates approached? All right, so I already knew the answer; a guy like Tristan wouldn't be caught dead seen with someone like me.

Sarah had rang me last night, informing me that she went out to the shops with Olivia, her two-year-older cousin, and guess who she ran into—Tristan. He was down there with his usual gang, and she apparently had enough courage to walk right up to them while in the food court and sit down, starting a conversation. I think it also helped that Olivia was there, and that she was just as pretty as Sarah was. She said she had a great time and couldn't understand why I had so many problems with those guys. I felt like screaming it was because they never did it when she was around. I guess they liked her too much to show their true side.

But I didn't bother explaining that to her; she knew how I felt about them, and it was up to her to think what she wanted.

In the end, she told me that when she said goodbye she leaned over the table and kissed Tristan again. My stomach dropped—why? She said the others started shouting and whistling their approval, and then she walked off.

Was I happy for her? Maybe. She seemed to really like Tristan. I did hope it could work out for them. Really, I did. Sort of.

I quickly showered and packed my bag for soccer late that afternoon.

Last year had been my final year for soccer because I wanted to concentrate on my studies, but Heather, the team captain, had called and asked if I could fill in for the day. I doubted I'd have enough time to get home after tutoring to change and drive back over to the indoor soccer field, which was a couple of blocks from the library, so I took my bag with me and headed out the door to work.

Dread filled me once more.

The two hours of work went quickly, and I managed not to make any mistakes. My head was tightly screwed onto my body, and my brain batteries were fully charged. In the last ten minutes, Michelle, a co-worker, turned up. She was the same age as me, only she attended another school and was really good-looking, tall and slim, with blonde hair, and light green eyes. And no matter what she wore, she always pulled it off; she had a thing for vintage clothing. I didn't know where she got them from, but they looked fantastic on her. I looked at her as she walked my way smiling, then I looked down at myself in pity. I was wearing my usual jeans and a t-shirt, which was the best thing for me to wear. Seemed like I couldn't pull off anything else. I was too short for any type of skirt, and I didn't fill out the front enough in dresses, so what did I have left? What I had on.

"Hey." Michelle winked. She came up really close and faced the opposite way from the front desk. "There's a guy sitting at the table in the far corner, and he keeps staring at you."

I looked over and locked gazes with Tristan. I hadn't even seen him come in, and usually I was attentive to when a person walked through the door. I liked to greet them on arriving. How long had he been there?

"Oh, that's just someone...ah, I—um..." I didn't think Tristan would want me to tell Michelle that he was here for me to tutor him. "He's a friend, ah, helping me with some school work."

She looked at me with a mischievous smile. "Oh, only a friend?"

"Yes." I nodded.

"Great! I can't go over there myself 'cause I have to take the desk now, but can you give him my number?" She slipped a piece of paper in my jeans pocket.

"Um, sure," I said and pushed my glasses up my nose.

"Thanks. You might as well go; it's just about time."

"Okay, thanks. Have a good rest of the day."

"I will, and don't forget." She gestured with her eyes to my pocket. I nodded at her and grabbed my bags from under the desk.

Tristan certainly received a lot of attention. He only had to walk past someone and they'd swoon his way. I wondered how many girlfriends he'd had. Or still did have.

"Hi," I said, placing my bags on the table with a thump.

He moved slightly, so I guessed that was a greeting. I opened the bag with my soccer gear in it and retrieved his jacket, which I'd stuffed in that morning.

"Thank you for that," I said, putting it on the table in front of him. He nodded and sat it in the seat next to him.

All right, we were full of words this morning. I sighed; this was going to be so much fun and comfortable. I was never really any good at sarcasm, and I felt bad once using it.

"Today we'll work on cosine ratio. Then next time we meet up, I thought we could revise on both ratios? Then if you feel comfortable with those, we'll move onto rational expressions, then factorization techniques, and finally variations. How does that sound?"

"You're the boss." He yawned.

"No, I'm here to help *you*. I need you to be all right with what I have set out, and then I need you to be honest with me. If you feel I'm going too fast, or if you want to work on something else, tell me, please."

"Yeah, all right; it's fine."

"Good."

I started explaining that cosine ratios were similar to tangent. He leaned forward in his seat once I started going through some examples. Then I wrote out some for him to work through. I could see him struggling with one, and I thought he was going to be too stubborn to ask me for help, but he wasn't. That was when I knew this arrangement was going to work. Tristan really did want to improve his grade, and it could be easy enough to do, because I knew if I explained it the right way, he caught on quickly. As he sat there next to me, working on the Maths homework we both had to get done before Monday, I had the chance to attempt my own homework from other subjects. I'd already done my Maths last night.

An hour-and-a-half later, I started packing up my things; if I didn't leave soon, I would be late for soccer. Tristan had only two problems to solve, so I was sure he'd be all right on his own.

"Sorry, Tristan, but I have to go."

He nodded his head while still going over the last problem. I took that as an okay and a goodbye included, so I got up from the table.

"Where are you going?" he asked, looking up at me.

"I just told you I have to go; I have to get to soccer down the road, and if I don't leave soon I'm going to be late."

"All right." He grabbed his own bag that held his homework, a pencil, and one notebook, and then stood up next to me. I looked at him curiously and started walking to the front door, waving at Michelle on the way, who tapped her front pocket.

I stopped out the front and turned to Tristan, he watched me reach into my pocket and pull out the piece of paper, which I thrust at him.

"Here."

He smirked at me. Did he really think it was from me?

"It's Michelle's number; the girl I work with in there. She asked me to give it to you."

"Really," he said, looking back through the library window. I glanced over as well to find Michelle there waving at him; he gave a chin lift back in greeting, which prompted Michelle to wink at him. He laughed. "Straight forward kinda girl."

"Yeah, I guess," I said, looking away.

"Like your other friend Sarah." He smiled down at me. And I meant *down* because I only came up to his chest.

"I'm shocked you remembered her name." My hand flew to my mouth. "Sorry." I blushed.

He rolled his eyes. "I saw her last night."

"I know. Look, I really have to go, so I guess I'll see you next Friday." I started to walk off when he called out.

"I'll see you Monday at school."

I couldn't stop the snort. "Maybe I should rephrase what I

just said. I'll see you at school, but I'll talk to you next Friday." With that, I walked off.

I wanted to turn around and apologise for sounding rude, but I didn't. Besides, he was the one who told me to stop apologising. Now all I had to do was stop feeling guilty about it.

Thankfully, I wasn't late. I had enough time to run into the locker rooms and change. I walked back out and onto feild one, and found Corbet sitting on the sidelines. I gave him a quick wave, surprised to see him, and went over to my team.

"Hey, girl, thanks for filling in," Heather greeted. She was the team captain and another friend of mine. Not that we did anything together on weekends or after school, but that was because we had different things in common. But ever since she confided in me about her troubles with her boyfriend last year, I found that we had connected on a different level.

Soon enough, the buzzer rang and the game started. I stood in my position as goalie. The team consisted of Heather, Serena, Danni, Wendy, and usually Sunny as their goalie. Sunny had taken over this year when I had quit, but she was sick.

We were in the second half when I heard a loud wolf whistle. I looked over to the side and found Sarah standing there smiling and waving. What I didn't expect was to see Tristan standing next to her.

Movement out the corner of my eye brought my attention back to the game as the other team drew closer, running with the ball. My team was fighting to get the ball back, but a burly player on the other team tripped Danni and bounded around her, still with the ball. She kicked it to the far left of the goal. I was standing to the far right. Before thinking, I flew sideways, arms outstretched to stop the ball as another team member of the other team ran right into me. Was it on purpose? I didn't know; all I did know was that I landed hard, my head taking most of the impact. The buzzer sounded. I looked behind me and found the ball in the goal. The other team had won.

Heather was at my side first, then Corbet, Tristan, and

Sarah, with the rest of the team and the referees. They all told me not to move, everyone asking me at the same time if I was okay.

I closed my eyes at their foolish question, because really, if I felt I was okay, I would have been on my feet by now.

All I could think about was the throbbing in my head.

Still, I needed to get up. I felt like a fool laying there with everyone around me. Even more of a fool because Tristan witnessed it. I sat up slowly with the help of Heather and Corbet.

"My glasses, are they broken?" I asked, holding my head at the same time.

"Here, they're fine," Tristan said, handing them over. I placed them on and found it helped my head a little. Only, I knew I was going to be sore for a while.

"You probably have a concussion," Corbet said.

Duh, was all I could think.

"All right, guys, let's clear the area," Heather demanded. The team disappeared; all that was left was Heather, Corbet, Sarah, and Tristan. What was he doing here?

"Corbet's right, Alex. You could have a concussion. Maybe you should go to the hospital," Heather said, concern showing on her face.

"NO! No, I'll be all right. No hospital."

"Well, someone's going to have to watch you tonight; your dad going to be home?"

"Yes, I'm sure he will be."

"Alex," Sarah warned.

"It's fine. Thanks, Heather." I smiled.

I got up slowly, only to feel dizzy. There was no way I was going to move with Heather still standing there; she was the type who would ring my house to make sure I was being taken care of. She'd make sure my dad would be home and tell him why he needed to be there. Only I was sure my dad wouldn't be home, and I would hate to disrupt his next case because of some silly bump on the head.

"Okay. Take care. Drink lots of fluids. I'll call you tomorrow."

I smiled and nodded. Bad choice. I had to grab my head after doing it. It made me feel nauseated. Heather gave me another concerned glance, turned, and thankfully left. I took a step forward and nearly fell over again. That was until Tristan caught me and straightened me up.

"What the hell are you doing here?" I growled and then gasped, my hand flying to my mouth. "Sorry, I really didn't mean that."

He laughed. "That's all right." He smiled. My stomach fluttered.

"I saw Tristan on the way here and asked him if he wanted to come with me. As you can see, he said yes." Sarah beamed.

"I don't think she needs to hear this right now," Corbet said through clenched teeth. "We need to get her home."

Sarah looked stricken. "Yes, of course. Luckily, we're staying at your house tonight, Alex. Someone needs to keep an eye on you." I rolled my eyes. "Do you think you can walk, or should Tristan carry you?"

"No! I'll be fine," I said quickly. "Only, I don't think I can drive my car home."

"Definitely not," Corbet agreed. "I'll drive it for you."

"But, Corbet, you came in your own car, and I came in mine. Tristan do you have your license?"

"Yeah, I can drive it," he said. Sarah rattled off my address for him.

"Great, you take Alex, and I'll go and grab her stuff while Corbet picks up some pizzas on the way to Alex's."

"Alex can come with me," Corbet said, glaring at Tristan. I knew he didn't trust Tristan, just like I hadn't, but now that I knew him, it was different. Wasn't it? Or was that just the head injury talking?

"But then she'd have to wait in the car for you to get pizza, when she should be home resting." Tristan smiled.

"Fine, whatever," Corbet said, and then left in a huff. Sarah gave Tristan a quick peck on the cheek, then left. Tristan placed his arm around my waist. I went to move away, but his grip tightened.

"You can barely stand on your own two feet; just let me help you."

I didn't meet his eyes. I was having a hard enough time trying not to blush from having his arm around me, while at the same time, trying not to throw up on him. So I nodded and leaned into him.

TWELVE

ALEXANDRA

Tristan had me wait out the front of the recreational centre as he ran off to collect my car. He sat me down on a bench near the road and wrapped his jacket around me. I told him not to bother, that I was fine, but that was when a shooting pain had me clutching at my head. He, of course, ignored me.

It was late in the afternoon, and it had turned a little chilly. So instead of cursing Tristan under my breath, I pulled his jacket closer around me while trying to hold it together. My head was killing me; what I needed was a double dose of pain medication and some sleep. Just as my eyes were drifting closed, I heard a car screech, a door slam, and loud pounding footsteps coming my way.

"Hey, Alex, this is no place to go to sleep, and you have to stay awake."

I opened my eyes as Tristan shook my shoulders.

"Just a little nap," I insisted.

He laughed and shook his head, which made me glare at him and curse him silently.

"Come on." He helped me stand and walked over to my car. How did he know which car was mine? I never told him. He opened the door and I lowered myself into the seat, and thanked anyone who cared that the car was warm. Still, I turned on my side and pulled Tristan's jacket tighter around me. He smelled wonderful.

"Um. Thanks, I guess," I muttered, half asleep.

"Alex, wake up." I felt something against my cheek. I opened my eyes to find that it was Tristan's hand gently tucking my hair behind my ear. "You have to stay awake, just for a little longer. Then you'll be home and can have some pain meds. Then you can sleep safely with someone watching you."

"Why are you being nice?" The question just popped out; I hadn't meant it to.

He scoffed. "I'm not that bad of a guy, am I?"

"Honestly, I can't comment; I don't know you." And I never really would once we were finished his tutoring. He fell quiet, so I took the opportunity to rest my eyes.

"Alex," he growled.

"Just resting, not sleeping," I said with my eyes closed.

"Open your eyes anyway. Then I'll know for sure."

I let out a sigh and opened them. "You're bossy, you know that?" I complained.

He laughed. "You only have to put up with it for a little longer."

I liked his laugh. It was deep, masculine, and it did things to me that I'd never felt before.

It's just the concussion talking.

"So, you and Corbet, hey?" I knew he was trying to distract me, keep me awake.

"So, you and Sarah, hey?" He looked over and smiled. I added, "Corbet and I are friends; not that it's any of your business."

"Well, I could say the same for Sarah and me."

"Sorry, doesn't work. It is my business because she's my friend, and I'll be the one picking up the pieces when you break her heart." And then, once again for the millionth time, I'd have to listen to her moaning and groaning about how she lost the love of her life. How he was such a good kisser...he couldn't be that good, could he? I looked to his nice manly lips and wondered what it would be like to have them on my own.

Definitely the concussion.

"What are you thinking about?"

I couldn't stop the blush and thanked, again, whoever would listen that he couldn't read minds. "Nothing," I replied.

"Well, we're here."

I turned my head slowly and looked out the front windscreen to see we were parked in my driveway and that my dad's car was, in fact, parked in front of mine. What was he doing home?

"My dad's home."

"You weren't expecting him?"

"No, he's usually working late."

"Even on weekends?"

"Any chance he can get." I turned back to Tristan. "Thank you for driving me home."

"Alex...will you be all right getting to the door?" It was obvious he was going to say something else, but changed his mind.

"Yes. I feel better now." He looked at me sceptically. "Really," I added. He raised his eyebrows. "Okay, fine, help me to the door. Besides, Sarah shouldn't be far away; you can stay for her. I'm sure she'll want to drive you home." He didn't say anything, but got out of the car and was around my side before I even had the chance to do anything. He opened the door, placed his hand under my arm, and helped me out. I swayed a little, but was happy I stayed on my own two feet. With the help of Tristan, that was.

"Alexandra?" Dad called from the front door. "What happened?" He came running over to grab my other arm.

"Nothing, Dad. Relax, I only hit my head in soccer."

"Hit it pretty hard," Tristan said.

Dad felt at the back of my head until he touched the sore spot and I hissed in pain. "You should go to the doctor."

"She refused," Tristan added.

"Thanks, Tristan. Dad, Tristan. Tristan, my father, Mr Harmony."

"Hello, Sir," Tristan said over my head because I was short enough for them to still see one another.

"Thank you for driving her home. Can I give you a lift somewhere?"

Wasn't that nice of him to offer?

"No, thanks anyway. I'm sure my lift will be here any minute," he said, and then smirked down at me. I rolled my eyes.

It wasn't even a second later that Sarah pulled up in her car, jumped out, and bound her way over to us.

"Hi, Mr H, didn't expect you to be home. Corby and I were going to stay the night and wake Alex up every half-hour to check on her."

"I'm not going anywhere tonight, but feel free to stay anyway. I'm sure Alex would prefer you and Corbet to wake her instead of her old man."

Or Tristan could? No. What was I thinking?

"You just don't want to be abused by her. We all know how crabby she can be when woken through the night."

"Really?" Tristan smiled.

"Okay, enough talking about me. All I want is to take something for this rotten headache and sleep; is that too much to ask? Or would you prefer to stand out here all night and talk about me like I'm not even here?" I grumbled.

"I can see it now." Tristan laughed, as did my dad. I elbowed Tristan in the ribs. He made an 'oof' sound and rubbed at his side like it actually hurt.

"Baby," I teased. "Sarah, Tristan wanted a lift home from you."

"Oh, sure." She beamed. Tristan's smile fell away.

"Thanks again for helping me," I offered. He nodded.

"Yes, thank you, Tristan. Come by any time."

DAAAD!

Tristan followed a skipping Sarah to her car as Dad helped me into the house and onto the couch.

"Don't close your eyes just yet, young lady. You need aspirin first. And really, I think you should go and see a doctor."

"You sound like Tristan. Dad, I'll be fine, honest."

"All right, sweetheart. Tristan seems like a nice lad."

"Yeah, I guess. He's Sarah's new conquer."

"Oh," he muttered.

Oh, what? Oh, that was a pity? Or oh, poor guy? But he didn't elaborate; he walked off to get me some aspirin. He came back quickly with his hand held out, my medication in it, and a glass of water.

"Thanks." I smiled. Once I took them, I moved enough to be comfortable and fell asleep right away.

᠅

I didn't know how much later it was, but I woke to a buzzing sound instead of someone shaking me like the last—too many to count—times. Only this time, the buzzing wouldn't stop like the shaking had when I yelled at them to go away. I rolled over on my bed, wondering how I got in my room in the first place, and reached for my phone to switch off the noise. Every time I received a text, it would buzz until I looked at it. What I really needed to do was learn how to put it on a timer to turn off on its own. I grabbed it, flipped it open, and fell back against my pillow, thinking of the past so many hours.

I remembered Corbet coming with pizza, because Dad had just woken me. He asked me if I wanted any; I told him to rack off and leave me alone. Something I wouldn't usually say. Then I remembered Sarah coming back because Corbet had just shaken me awake as she walked through the front door.

When my dad woke me the last time before my annoying phone had, I could hear Corbet and Sarah talking in the background, which meant they stayed. While I waited for my brain to defog so I could read the text, I looked over the edge of my bed to find them on the usual double mattress, sleeping soundly. Sarah lay on her stomach, closest to my side of the bed, and Corbet was on his back, his mouth open and small sounds coming from him. I was lucky enough that my phone hadn't woken them; they would have been tired, for obvious reasons. I glanced at the clock and found it was six in the morning. Who would be texting this early?

I rolled onto my side and pressed a button to light up my phone to see who the rude person was. It read that I had five new messages. I opened the inbox and found that I had three from a number I didn't know, and two from Heather. I quickly read through the ones from Heather; in the first one she was asking how I was. When I didn't reply the first time, the next one said,

You better answer me before I ring your house so late.

She must have rang because she hadn't sent anymore.

The other three read:

Alexandra, hope you r feeling better!

Did ur dad take you to doctors? Wait, prob not 'cause u can be stubborn :)

And the last one that was from six in the morning:

Just realised you wouldn't have known who the messages b4 r from. It's Tristan. Have a nice SAFE day :)

A smile spread across my face, and butterflies took over my stomach. I was glad that my phone hadn't woken up Corbet or Sarah, because if I'd had this reaction in front of them, then they'd be pestering me about who they were from, causing Sarah to be hurt, and I didn't want that. I would never intentionally hurt her.

I wasn't sure if I should reply, but then if I did, maybe he would send another back to me. With a shaking hand, I replied.

What r u doing awake this early? AND I AM NOT STUBBORN!!

I waited and waited, and then remembered to turn my phone to silence just before I received:

Hows head?? U R Stubborn! I'm workin'.

My fingers flew over the phone:

Head okay. I'm alive if that counts. What work u doing?

Seconds later, he sent:

It does count. Deliveries. Next time U drive me home, no matter what condition ur in. I'm sure I'd be safer. S crazy driver!!

I couldn't *not* laugh; I knew what he was talking about. I even hated getting in a car with Sarah.

Ha. Deal. Better let u get back to work—slacker x

I'd already hit send before I reread it. I had automatically put an x on the end like I'd always done with Sarah, and now it was too late to take it back. Was it just me, or had it taken longer for him to reply? Would he even reply after my stuff up? My phone vibrated in my hand, making me jump. I opened it:

Have a good day Alexandra!

I smiled again; he either didn't notice it, or he didn't think anything by it. I hoped both.

Sighing, I rolled over to my other side, my gaze falling on Sarah. Would she be angry that I was just texting her guy? Probably. And for that, I felt guilty.

Now I regretted texting him back. No matter if it brought a smile to my face or that it made me feel warm inside. I had to remember that we were just...what?

Nothing really, I was a guide for him through Maths. Perhaps we could become friends if he and Sarah went further. Other than that, it would have to be nothing. Too many painful things could happen from becoming too close to him.

THIRTEEN

ALEXANDRA

Dad forced me to stay home Monday. I said I felt fine to attend school, but he was using his stern voice, so I didn't argue. At least it gave me some time to finish homework and start on the two assignments I had to get done for English and Science.

After four hours of doing just that, I'd had enough. My mind kept travelling off to Tristan and I couldn't explain why. It was as though he'd taken over my brain. Sure, I'd had crushes before, but this felt different to those. Was it a crush at all? Or was it just the fact that I liked his company for some reason? But how could that be when I knew for certain that if his so-called friends found out we were spending time together, he'd never admit to it. He'd feel ashamed of being associated with me.

Why was he so nice to me then?

His friends were so different; they were obnoxious jerks. What did Tristan see in them? What did they talk about? Did he do the same as they did when he was with them? I hadn't the answers, and that frustrated me even more.

So how could I think that I may like him, when really I didn't know him?

And anyway, I couldn't like him. Sarah had her claws stuck

into him already. I would never go behind her back just for a guy.

Listen to me; it's as if I thought I had a chance in the first place.

I didn't. He was way out of my league and I had to remember it.

It had to be infatuation, and once our time together drew to an end, I'd get over it. Things would go back to as they were…as they should be.

I flopped back on my bed and sighed loudly. I didn't like this feeling, being this discombobulated. I had always known what I wanted, and I strived to get just that. But with Tristan, I didn't know where I was at.

My phone buzzed beside me; I expected it to be Dad checking up on me, which he shouldn't feel the need to when I told him that I felt fine that morning. I sat up and reached for my phone on my bedside table, flipping it open to read the message.

How r u feeling?

My breath caught. I didn't recognise the number at first, and I hadn't saved it into my phone in case…well, in case Sarah happened to look through it one day. I didn't want to explain why I was receiving messages from her boyfriend.

The question was: should I reply? Then again, I was never one to be rude. So I opted to type back something short.

Fine thank you.

He replied quickly.

I'm sitting in Maths bored out of my brain

I smiled at that and sent my response.

Can't say I'm missing it. U should be concentrating, then u won't need my help.

Tristan replied.

U coming tomorrow?

I wondered for a brief moment if he missed me, then shook my head at myself as I typed back a short answer.

Prob.

After a few seconds, he sent a simple message.

C U.

Bye.

I typed and pressed the send button.

Why would he text me? Maybe he'd like to be friends? And then, I went and turned around, having inappropriate thoughts about him. Well, no more of that.

The rest of the week went quickly. I was right about one thing: whenever I saw Tristan in class or down the hallway at school, he acted like he didn't know me. I wasn't surprised by this; it wasn't as though I expected him to ditch his idiot friends and come hang with us.

Sarah had enough confidence to go up to him on Friday at lunch while he was sitting in the cafeteria with his friends and ask him what his plans were for the weekend. I could hear Tristan's friends taunting them both. Sarah kept her head held high and teased them back. She told me later that he wasn't doing much, and that she'd asked him to the movies. His reply was 'maybe'.

As she'd been talking to him, though, I couldn't stop myself from looking over and met his gaze; we both quickly looked away.

Friday afternoon, I walked into the library expecting to see Mrs Doherty, but found Michelle standing behind the counter.

"Hey, girlfriend." She smiled. "Mrs D is sick, so she called me in. I needed the extra money anyway 'cause I wanted to buy this pair of knee-high boots that would totally look so cute on me. They may seem out of it with my usual attire, but I can't resist them. It's like they call to me. So what's been happening with you? Oh, and that hottie you were with last Sat is sitting over there." My heart started beating wildly. She pointed across the room to the table in the far corner. Tristan was already here? Why?

He had texted me twice over the week, but I couldn't bring myself to reply to him. I wanted to; my fingers itched to do it. But then, I knew my mind would wander off with more inappropriate thoughts regarding him, and I was having a hard enough time trying not to do that. Did I feel bad for not texting back? Yes I did; like I have said before, I wasn't one who liked to be rude. But the more I thought about it, the more it made sense that he'd be better off with diverting his niceness to Sarah.

When he looked up from whatever he was doing, I gave a small wave; he gave me a chin lift and stared back down at his books. Was he actually here to study? That was good to see.

I spent my two hours of work helping customers with borrowing or returning their items. Michelle took it upon herself to go out into the library, placing the returned books back on the right shelves. Every now and then between customers I would look over to Tristan, and sometime catch him looking back. A couple of times, Michelle would be there, charming her way into his life.

Finally, work finished for me. Michelle came back over to the desk and took over my position. The rest of the returns would be left for someone else to do in the morning—mainly me—although, if Tristan turned up early tomorrow, I knew Michelle would appoint herself to be on floor duty again, even though she hated it.

"Damn, girl, he is fine." Michelle sighed and leaned against the corner of the desk.

"He's okay, I suppose. Ah…what were you two talking about?"

"Nothing much, just bands we like to go and watch. I found out we both like Maiden Marriage. I told him they're playing at Joe's Pool Hall next weekend and asked him if I'd see him there. Even told him I'd make it worth his while—"

"You didn't!" I squeaked.

She gave me a sly smile back and nodded. "But all he said was he'll see. Can you make sense of that, girl? Anyway, he said he was here to see you, doing some work together or something. So if you can, you know, put in a good word for me?"

"I'll try," I said, grabbing my bag from under the counter and walking over to the table before she could say anything else.

"Hey." Tristan smiled as I reached him.

"Hello. You've been here a while."

"Yeah, I've been doing some homework so I can have spare time to do other things on the weekend."

I smiled at him while getting the books out of my bag. "Too bad you have to come back here tomorrow."

"It isn't so bad," he said, looking confused. He glanced over my shoulder. Oh, he must have meant that Michelle was here for him to admire.

"Yes. Well, she asked me to put in a good word for her with you."

"Who?" His brows drew together.

"Michelle."

He snorted and shook his head. "She's not my type."

"Sarah, then? No, forget I said that."

He laughed. "She's an okay sort of girl. She asked me out to the movies this weekend, but I'm sure I didn't have to tell you that."

"No." I smiled.

"How come you didn't reply to my texts?"

My heart stuttered; I honestly thought he wouldn't bring it up. "I...well, you see...it's Sarah. I don't know. I thought that, um, she would hate it if she found out you and I...that we were communicating behind her back...and I would tell her, only she will get jealous. I think. She really likes you and I felt guilty. I would hate to think that I could upset her. I would have texted you otherwise. I...um, wanted to, but you see it's just..."

"Sarah," he supplied.

"Yes."

"Do you always worry so much? Put other people before yourself?"

I looked away and blushed; was I that obvious? "Yes, I do."

"I thought so. Anyway, what have you got planned for us tonight?" Why did that sound so good to my ears, especially coming from his mouth? I blushed again and fumbled through explaining my thoughts. I caught him smirking at my bumbling.

It wasn't until sometime later that I remembered we were supposed to be revising both ratios, and I'd already moved on to rational expressions. I could have hit my head for being so forgetful.

And an utter fool.

At the end of our time together, I said, "You've done well tonight." I smiled. He returned it, which made my stomach flutter.

I was only hungry.

"I've had a good teacher."

"Thank you." I blushed.

He laughed. "Is it always this easy to get your cheeks warm?"

"Usually, yes."

He chuckled. "Are you always honest?"

I looked at him and held his gaze. "I try to be."

"Good to know. So do you think I should go out with Sarah tomorrow night?" He raised his right eyebrow at me.

No! Would have been my first answer, but I couldn't do that. "Are you testing my honesty approach here?"

He grinned. "I could be."

I shook my head at him and looked down at the table. "You really confuse me, Tristan."

"That wasn't an answer to my question though."

I smiled, glanced at him, then away. "No, I guess it wasn't."

"I've also noticed that you're good at avoiding topics when you don't like them. So will you answer me, Alex?"

I sighed, but still didn't look at him. Some people have said they could tell what I was thinking by just looking into my eyes. "I think that it is up to you." There.

He laughed. "Very diplomatic of you. I'd better go; I'll see you tomorrow."

I looked at him and nodded. He left the table without another word. I deflated in my seat. What I wanted was for him to stay, to talk some more, and to get to know him. Not that I should. My phone beeped inside of my jacket, I flipped it open, a smile spreading across my face. I looked around, but I couldn't see him anywhere. I looked back down at my phone and read it again.

It's only a text Alex. She should understand that. Would you feel better if I started texting her?

No, I wanted to scream, but I found myself typing back.

Yes.

I knew that would be ur answer so I already have. We r going to the movies tomorrow night. R u happy?

Why would he ask me that? Everything in me told me that I wasn't happy. When I read what he'd written, I felt a sinking feeling in the pit of my stomach. And for some silly reason, I felt like crying. I felt that I'd missed out and that wasn't fair.

But did I really have a right to feel that way? No.

It did seem that Tristan wanted to be friends, a friend who asked dating advice, I guess. And even if it was a secret friendship so his other idiot mates didn't find out, I could be fine with that. Because I already knew I wouldn't like it if Tristan disappeared out of my life completely.

Alex?

I couldn't bring myself to answer that though. So instead, I changed the subject completely and asked a question that had been on my mind, which would lead me to get to know more things about him.

How many siblings do you have?

:) Three. Two older twin brothers, but one passed away last year. And an older sister who lives two hours away.

I closed my eyes for a second before responding.

I'm sorry for ur loss. I know how it feels; it's hard. Always will be I think for the rest of our lives.

Everyone usually says: with time it will get better, but not you.

I hate that saying! I've heard it many times myself. I guess because I've been through it I know the truth.

New question time, other stuff too depressing. Who do you work for?

:(depressing is my thing though, but all right. Sam's Deliveries, just like a postal service, I deliver the things that are too big for letterboxes.

I imagined him lifting heavy boxes with his muscles flexing before I shook myself out of it and replied.

Interesting. How many girlfriends hav u had?

Oh. My. God. Had I really texted that? Yes, yes I had. My heart was beating like crazy.

Why so u can warn S?

No, just curious.

Two serious ones. U?

How embarrassing; I knew I shouldn't have asked.

Zero.

Really???

Honest remember? No hassling though.

I wouldn't. Better go, just met up with the guys.

Maybe I shouldn't have told him; I immediately regretted it. Would he tell the other guys? I doubted it because he wouldn't talk about me in the first place. Was it going to be awkward tomorrow? Probably, and I only had myself to blame.

Stuff honesty.

Saturday morning, I woke to find my phone flashing as I rolled over stretching. I opened it up and read the text from Tristan. It said that he couldn't make it today; he had to do something for his mom.

Groaning, I hit my bed. I knew I shouldn't have said anything. I should never have thought that we could have that type of friendship. I didn't know what I was doing. But I did know the texting had to stop, and no more personal questions.

FOURTEEN

ALEXANDRA

I went to work at the library like normal, but still couldn't help myself from looking to the back corner at the table Tristan and I usually sat at. Just to see if he'd managed to get out of whatever his mom had asked him to do. That was, if he hadn't lied in the first place.

Every time I did look and saw he wasn't there, it made me a little more disappointed and a little more upset with myself—for being so open with him in the first place.

After work finished, I went straight to my bag, and opened my phone to check it, letting out a sigh when I saw nothing. Besides the message from Corbet saying he'd be late tonight. He decided he was still going to stay even though Sarah wouldn't be there, because Sarah would be out on a date with Tristan.

"Whoa there, girlfriend, easy on the phone before you break it with that super grip you have going on."

I looked down at my hand. I did indeed have a tight grip on the phone; I lessened it, turned it off, and threw it into my bag. *I am not turning it on again until tomorrow, or even Monday,* I told myself, hoping I would actually listen.

"Hey, where's your spunky friend today?" Michelle asked.

This was the first chance we had to speak all day; it had been really busy.

"He had other things he needed to do."

"Did he tell you the other day that he texted me? I was so excited until he said he already had a girlfriend. How come you didn't tell me that part?"

"It's only new; I didn't think it was official yet."

So he was now calling Sarah his girlfriend.

"Oh, well, that's cool if it's only new." She looked over her shoulder to the waiting customer. "I better get back to work. Have a good rest of the weekend, girl."

"Thank you and you too." I smiled, grabbed my bag, and walked out into the cool afternoon air.

During the drive home, I listened to the new CD I had bought a couple of weeks ago by Adele; her voice was so strong and beautiful. I pulled into my driveway and found that my dad's car was there. As I was walking into the house, Dad was making his way out the door carrying an arm-full of case notes. I tried to move out of his way in time, but it was obvious his mind was on other matters, and he still managed to collide with me.

"Ah shoot," he said as the case notes floated to the ground. "Sorry, honey I didn't see you there."

"That's all right, Dad. New case I presume?" I asked, bending to help him pick them all up.

"Yeah, and right now, I wish I hadn't taken it on. Look, it's going to be a very long night. I've left some money on the counter for you guys to grab some takeaway. No driving after eight, and no scary movies; I know what they do to you." He was down the stairs on his way to the car when he yelled over his shoulder, "Say hi to Sarah and Corbet for me. Love you, hon. Be good."

"Always am." I smiled. I didn't have the heart to inform him it was only Corbet staying tonight.

I still had a fair amount of time to kill before Corbet arrived and we'd head off to the video store and grab some takeaway. So I chose to do the only thing that kept my mind busy and didn't start thinking about other things that started with the letter T. I got out my workbooks from school and began my homework.

Around six, I was in the kitchen folding the clothes I'd gotten off the line when the doorbell rang. I was thinking that it had to be Corbet arriving early, but as I opened the door, my hand flew to my mouth to hide the gasp and startled cry wanting to escape.

Tristan stood on the other side, only he looked a little worn. He was leaning against the doorframe with a pained expression. Any wonder with that cut on his lip, an already-bruised cheek, and his black tee had tears in it.

"Oh, my God, Tristan, what happened? Are you okay? That was a stupid question. Come in here now." I grabbed his arm and dragged him over the threshold, proceeding on into the kitchen where I sat him down in a kitchen chair, raising his face up to the light to get a better look.

I *tsked* at him and shook my head. "How did this happen, Tristan? No, wait, let's get you cleaned up first." I went over to the kitchen sink, to the cupboard under it, and grabbed out the first aid kit. Then I filled a bowl with warm water and grabbed a rag off one of the piles I'd already folded.

I stood in front of him, placing the bowl and kit on the table. After wringing out the rag, I grabbed his chin so he would look up again.

"It's not as bad as it looks. Just a few scratches," he said, wincing when his lip cracked and started to bleed.

"I'll be the judge of that, thank you." As gently as I could, I placed the towel on his lip; he didn't even flinch.

Once the bleeding had stopped, I moved onto the scratch he had in his hairline above his left eye. One I hadn't noticed the first time I saw him. Again, as gently as I could, I wiped away the dried blood. I opened the first aid kit, searching through it, saying, "Huh, huh…" when I found what I was looking for, the antiseptic cream.

"This is going to hurt," I apologised.

"It's all right," he said, rolling his eyes.

"First, are you going to tell me what happened?"

"Not likely."

"I thought so. Just…if you ever want to talk, I'm here." I didn't wait for a response. Instead, I dabbed his lip with the cream I'd applied to my finger. He let out a small hiss, then nothing, staying perfectly still. I moved onto his forehead and then realisation hit me—how close I was standing to him, how his warmth seemed to reach out to me, how his legs must have automatically spread for me to be standing in between them. I blushed, quickly finished, and stepped back.

"All d—done," I stuttered. "Unless, of course, there's some-where else." I laughed. He didn't laugh with me, only looked into my eyes and then removed his tee.

Lord Almighty, what a sight it was.

I knew he was built, but nothing could prepare me for the washboard six-pack, pumped chest, and glorious-looking, soft caramel skin. Once again, I blushed and looked away quickly from his smirking face.

"I, ah…I don't see anything."

"On my back, Alexandra." He chuckled.

I walked around him and gasped. "Oh, they're beautiful."

He looked over his shoulder, seeming confused. "What, the cuts?"

"No, I…um, I mean your tattoos." His whole upper back was covered in scrolls. I couldn't help myself. I reached out with one finger and traced some of them until my brain registered what I was doing. "Sorry," I uttered, pulling my hand away.

"It's fine." His voice sounded deeper, almost like a growl.

I busied myself with the task at hand. I went back over to the sink, emptied the already-bloodied water, and refilled it with some fresh warm water, while rinsing the rag under the flowing stream. Without making eye contact, I walked back to his stunning back. Because I knew if I did happen to meet his gaze, that I would blush again, which he'd find amusing.

I wrung out the towel and began on one of the four cuts he had on his lower back. Like his forehead, they'd already dried, so it was going to be harder to get that blood off. He was kind enough to let me work in silence and admire his bare skin while doing it. Even though I had a million and one questions burning away inside of me, I didn't ask any. If he wanted to tell me, he would in his own time, if at all.

I was on the last one, applying the antiseptic cream and healing tape over them so they wouldn't be sticky for him when he placed his tee back on.

Why had he come here?

Upon finishing, and again, without thinking, I leaned over and placed a gentle kiss on his shoulder.

"All done," I said. Then gasped, my hand flying to my mouth. I slowly stood up straight and took a step away.

"Stop." Tristan growled. He was mad at me for doing what I just did; I couldn't blame him. I didn't know what came over me; it was just automatic.

"I—um, I'm really sorry," I couldn't look at him; I continued studying the floor. "I don't know why I did that. God, I'm so, so sorry. It won't happen again;, not that I think that you'd be hurt again and come here for me to patch you up, but you know. I mean, I won't get all up in your personal space..."

"Alexandra." Tristan sighed.

"Sorry," I squeaked.

His feet moved into my view on the floor—gulp— meaning he was standing right in front of me. Still, I couldn't handle looking into his eyes. All I wanted to do was crawl under my bed and die of embarrassment.

He grabbed my chin in a gentle grip and pulled my face up to meet his intense gaze. Only it didn't work, I managed to look anywhere but at him. He let out another sigh and placed both hands on each side of my face, stopping my head from moving, so I closed my eyes.

"Damn it, Alexandra, look at me."

Boy, did he sound mad.

I reluctantly opened my eyes. He already had my neck cranked up so I would be looking straight at him. He didn't look so mad, but he had definitely sounded like it before.

"Only you call me Alexandra. Well, besides my dad, but it sounds better coming out of your mouth..." I bit my bottom lip before I could say anything else that I would regret.

He smiled down at me. "Thank you for taking care of me—"

"Well, I didn't really do anything; it's just lucky I already had the kit under the sink, because my dad always informs me that you can't be too careful; you always should have a first aid kit in the house. So at least he's right about one thing. Oh, I don't mean that he's always wrong, because he's not, just sometimes he can be a little overprotective—"

"Alexandra," Tristan barked. Not that his bark stopped my rambling, it was when one of his fingers ran along my bottom lip. "Can't you just let me thank you without having you rattle on about nothing?"

"That's a bit rude; it wasn't about nothing. I was explaining to you about how my dad—"

"I guess not." He chuckled. He removed my glasses, placed them on the table beside us, and slowly lowered his face to mine. His lips headed right for my own. He smiled when he witnessed my eyes widen in shock, then his lips touched mine, and every sane thought left my body.

I wrapped my arms around his shoulders and pulled him tighter, hearing a moan escape him, which made me feel pleased about myself. For some reason, I thought that it was too gentle for my liking, not that I wasn't really enjoying myself. I was shocked with myself to find that I wanted to pull myself up higher, and wrap my legs around his waist so I could bring him as close as I could to me. That was, until I remembered he had a sore lip and the front doorbell chimed.

I pulled away from him. "Snap," I cursed.

Tristan laughed, pulling me close again into his embrace. "You cannot tell me that was your first kiss."

That made me laugh and blush. "Well no, but you're only the second."

"Hmm, I think I like that." He grinned a big toothy grin, which made my insides curl.

There was a bang on the door. "Come on, Alex, open up. I am not in the mood to be left out here much longer."

Double snap, Sarah.

"Oh, my God." I gasped and stepped away from Tristan. "That's Sarah. Snuffle it! Aren't you supposed to be on a date with my best friend?" I slapped my forehead with my hand and looked in the direction of the front door. "Oh God, did you stand her up? Did you at least text her. She's going to hate me."

"Alex," Tristan said, grabbing my hand with his so I'd turn back to him. "She doesn't have to know about what just happened. Look, I'll sneak out the back door and text her if that will make you feel better. But what I don't want you doing is feel sorry for that kiss. Besides, it was a thank you kiss, that's all."

Sniffing to hold back my emotions, a tear escaped that I didn't know was threatening to come out. He wiped it away, pulling me into his arms again. I lay my head against his chest.

"I know." I did know it was a thank you kiss, and that made me feel a little hurt. "And I won't, I mean, feel sorry about it," I uttered. How could I when it was the best kiss I'd ever had. I felt his head nod.

Another pound at the door. "Open up, Alex." This time it was Corbet.

Tristan sighed. "All right, I better go before they break the door down. I guess I'll see you at school?"

I looked up at him and stepped back. "Yeah." I smiled, even though I felt sick inside. Had I just betrayed my friend's trust?

"Here, take this." I threw one of Dad's t-shirts at him; he pulled it on, gave me one last look, and left out the back door of the kitchen.

After tidying the kitchen quickly, I went to open the front door. Silently praying for help because I wanted to cry. I wanted to follow Tristan and yell at him for making me feel things that he obviously wasn't. But what I prayed for the most was for help to get through the night without having them questioning me about...anything. I was afraid I was going to break—about Tristan and for feeling like I'd just betrayed Sarah.

I closed my eyes. Oh God, that kiss was a thank you kiss and nothing else.

There I went again, confusion, feelings, and for what—a thank you kiss?

What had me more upset than anything was wondering if that kiss would have happened in the first place if he hadn't come here? Because really, in the real world, I couldn't see that occurring. I was not his type. Just plain, boring, nerdy, old me, with stupid glasses.

I wanted to scream in frustration. Instead, I plastered on a smile and opened the door.

FIFTEEN

ALEXANDRA

The first two days of school dragged; my mind wasn't on education—it kept thinking of Tristan, Sarah, and the situation I'd put myself in. After Sarah and Corbet had walked in Saturday night, Sarah's phone started ringing. She answered it, and I could hear Tristan's deep voice on the other end, but I couldn't make out what he was saying. Not that I had to; once Sarah got off the phone smiling from ear to ear, she told me what had been said: that he'd rung to apologise that he hadn't made it to their date because he had some troubles at home. Of course, she understood. So they planned to make another arrangement to catch up after school Tuesday night.

My stomach had dropped at that point, and as I sat in Maths on Wednesday, with Tristan in the back with his mates, I wondered how it went last night. I wondered if they kissed, what they talked about, or where they went.

I found myself feeling slightly jealous, and I shouldn't. I had no right to. I just had to keep reminding myself that what happened between Tristan and I was only a thank you kiss. It didn't mean anything else, and nothing else would come from it.

He was with Sarah, and she seemed happy. I would do nothing to take that away from her.

I thought she would have called me last night to fill me in about her date, but she hadn't. Then I thought I would have seen her this morning and she would have told me all about it then, but I didn't. So that was why I was in Maths, chewing the end of my pencil. My mind was off spending time pondering on what had occurred last night instead of on the class. Had he had fun? Maybe she got back too late to call me? Maybe she slept in because of such a late night? If that was the case, what had them staying out so late?

Arhahah. I really wanted to scream out loud.

"Miss Harmony, are you with us today?" Mrs Doherty asked, breaking through my unwanted thoughts.

"Yes, yes, please continue." People laughed. I realised what I'd said and looked up to see Mrs Doherty's glare.

"Thank you for the permission, Miss Harmony. I'd like to see you after class."

I had never heard those words come out of a teacher's mouth. Sorry, I had heard them, only not addressed to me. I nodded, sunk lower in my seat, and tuned into what she was talking about.

The bell rang and I stayed seated. I watched the class file out for lunch and Tristan glanced over his shoulder at me; he was smiling as he walked out. What was he smiling at?

The teacher was concerned about my attitude. I told her it was never going to happen again, that my mind was on other things. She nodded and sighed, then asked me how Tristan and I were doing studying together. That brought a smile to my face and I informed her that things were coming along in strides. She agreed that things had improved in his work and thanked me for taking my time out to help him.

I made my way to the cafeteria. I wasn't really in the mood to eat, but as I sat down at the table with Sarah and Corbet, I grabbed out an apple and started munching on it.

"Well?" Sarah asked.

I looked up at her grinning face and asked, "Well what?"

She sighed. "Don't you want to know how my date went?"

No! "Yeah, of course I do," I said, making myself smile.

"Not really," Corbet muttered.

Sarah ignored him and went on. "It was fantastic; we went out to tea at Benny's—you know, the seafood place? We talked and talked for hours. He asked me if I wanted to go to the movies after. I told him I couldn't, that I had to get home by curfew. But that didn't stop us from making out for the next two hours in my car. He is such a good kisser. I think I may be falling in love with him."

Both Corbet and I choked. Corbet on his drink, and me on my apple. Right from the start, I felt sick with every word she'd said, but now, I really thought I was going to throw up.

My hand went to my mouth and I excused myself from the table, running out to get to the bathroom in time.

Thankfully, I made it, only nothing came up. After retching for a while, I went to the sink and splashed water on my face; it helped a little, but the nauseous feeling wouldn't go away. Maybe I was really getting sick, or was it the thought of Tristan and Sarah together.

How could one boy make me so crazy?

It didn't matter; somehow, I had to get him out of my head. He belonged with Sarah. In more ways than one.

I went through the rest of the day like a zombie; in the end, my art teacher told me to go home because I looked pale and didn't want anyone else catching anything. On my way out, I texted Sarah and Corbet, telling them both that I wasn't feeling well and I'd see them tomorrow.

I got home to an empty house—nothing unusual there. I went to run a nice warm bath, hoping it would relax me and take the stress away that I was causing my own self.

It had, and it wasn't until I was in my room getting dressed into tracksuit pants and a jumper that I heard two voices coming from the kitchen.

"Dad?" I called.

"Hi, honey. I finished early so I thought I'd get take-out for us. Come and eat."

I stomped out into the kitchen and froze. Leaning against the bench was Tristan.

"What are you doing here?" I hissed.

"Alex," Dad said sternly.

"Sorry. It's…uh, I just thought you worked Wednesday nights?"

Like Tuesday nights!

"I have a couple of days off while it's quiet," he explained, a smile tugging at his lips.

"I saw Tristan down the street while getting Chinese. He asked how you were feeling after leaving school; I said I didn't know you were unwell. How are you feeling?"

"Better," I told Dad, and then asked Tristan, "How did you know?"

He shrugged and said, "Sarah."

Of course. I nodded and looked to the floor.

"I asked Tristan to eat with us. I hope that's okay."

I shrugged and then shook my head and said, "Well, I'm sick. I mean, I'd hate anyone else to catch it."

"Cooties never bothered me." Tristan smiled. The look in his eyes made me blush. I nodded and sat at the table.

Tristan and my father kept the conversation going through dinner. I sat silently and listened to them talking about work, sports, family (mainly his), and then Dad brought up the subject of Sarah. I could not believe it.

"So how are things with Sarah going? I mean, I know she's a handful—"

"Dad," I yipped, but Tristan just laughed.

"It's all right, Alex. I admit, she *is* full on, but we're only at the start, so who knows."

"Good luck with it anyway."

"Dad!"

I was appalled. Dad had never understood my relationship

with Sarah. He saw the huge difference between us. But I was never one to knock back a friendship; it was hard for me to make them in the first place, so who was I to argue when Sarah chose Corbet and me to spend time with?

Dad cleared his throat. "Anyway, I'll clean up here; how about you take Tristan into the lounge? I'm sure he'd like to watch that football game that's on."

"I'm sure Tristan has better things to do," I said as I stood from the table.

"No, not really. A football game sounds good." He got up from the table and followed me into the formal lounge.

"Take him into the other lounge; it has a bigger television, Alexandra," Dad yelled.

I let out a sigh and went down to the back of the house where the comfortable lounge was. Where Sarah, Corbet, and I loved watching our DVDs. I flopped down onto the couch, leaving Tristan to pick from many other chairs, but he sat next to me. Pulling my legs up, I wrapped my arms around them and turned on the television to find the right channel.

Quietly, I sat there; I could feel Tristan's gaze on me, but I refused to meet it. Why had he accepted my dad's invitation for dinner? This was the last thing I needed when I already couldn't get him out of my head.

Stuff that stupid thank you kiss.

Because all I could think when picturing that kiss in my mind was an image of him and Sarah together. All those warm, fuzzy feelings I had for him were soon squished, and instead it left me angry and sick.

"Alex."

"Yes."

"Have I made you upset for being here?"

I looked down at my knees and mentally groaned. Even though the guy was driving me insane inside, I didn't want him to think that I didn't like his company. It was my own fault for getting stupid feelings for him in the first place.

Sighing, I said, "No. I know we're friends and friends come to each other's place. So no, I get it. Only, I think I'm going to have to tell Sarah about it, and at least it was my dad inviting you over. I didn't do it—I mean, not that I wouldn't have. Actually, I don't know if I would have, but it just makes it easier for me to tell Sarah, and then at least she shouldn't be upset with me, right?" I asked and then shook my head. "No, she shouldn't."

"Why do you care so much if you upset her? It's like you worry about what she'd do."

"No, no, that's not it. I mean, it is; of course it is. I do care if I upset her; that's what friends do, right? I'd even hate it if I upset Corbet in any way."

I was not a bad person; I'd rather hurt myself than anyone else.

"Do you want me to leave?"

"No. Unless, you want to. It's not like I don't enjoy your company; I do. So I'll just get over my hang-ups and we can just go along like we have been. I think I'll feel better once Sarah knows that we're friends."

"You're one strange girl, Alexandra."

I sighed and nodded. "I know. It's just weird, you know, you being here, and that we've become friends, and that you're dating my friend."

And that we kissed and I couldn't stop thinking about it, about you. But I had to.

"You say 'friends' a lot." He smiled. I looked over at him and laughed; he laughed with me and it made me feel better, more relaxed. "And Sarah and I aren't dating; we've only been out once."

"Don't let Sarah hear you say that; in her eyes, one date is enough to say that the two of you are dating."

"We'll see." He grunted. I couldn't help but giggle. Yes, he would see and then find out that I was right. "What are you laughing at?" he asked.

"Oh, nothing. So tell me, Tristan, do you really like football?"

I glanced over at him as he shrugged his shoulders and then said, "It's okay. I'm more of a hockey guy, though. So tell me, Alexandra, what's up with you and Corbet?"

"Like I've said before, there's nothing going on. We *are* just friends, and in my eyes, that's all we ever will be. I could never see him any other way. I've known him for what seems like forever. Wait, let me guess, Sarah's said something." When he grinned and raised his eyebrows at me, I knew I was right. I groaned and shook my head. "Of course she has. She has this weird thought that Corbet likes me, but I highly doubt it. If anything, I think it was the other way around, that he likes her —" I grabbed his arm. "Not that you need to worry about it. He knows where he stands with her…with both of us." I quickly let go when he looked down at my grip on his hand. "Anyway, quick change in subject, do you want to play the Wii?"

He laughed again at how frustrated I seemed, which I was. What was Sarah doing talking about me to Tristan? I was sure she'd have better things to talk about, and if all else failed, she would just have to stick her tongue down his throat—*God, that sounded terrible.* I couldn't believe I even thought it.

"The Wii sounds good, but only for a short while, and then I'm going to have to go."

"All right." I got up to change the cables and grab the remotes. While changing the channel over and walking backwards, I tripped over Tristan's feet, which planted me right into his lap. I scrambled to get up as he tried helping me by placing his hands under my arms, but that only made it worse.

I gasped and said, "Don't—stop! I'm ticklish there." And I knew as soon as those words were out of my mouth that I would regret them.

I was halfway up when he started moving his fingers under my arms. I squealed and wriggled, laughter bursting from my mouth. "Please, no, oh, stop!" I begged and giggled like a little girl. He was chuckling at me squirming around, trying to get away from him.

"What's all the noise?" Dad asked, coming into the lounge.

Tristan froze, moved to sit back down. I quickly got up off the floor and straightened myself out.

"Oh, I see you've found her weak spot. Let me tell you, it works wonders when she's arguing with me. All I have to do is tickle her there and she caves." Dad smiled at the many memories when he had used those tactics on me.

"Yes, not fair at all," I uttered with a mock scowl and sat back down on the couch. Tristan seemed to relax from our light words, knowing that my dad wouldn't have jumped to the wrong conclusions by what he'd seen.

"Hey, you guys playing the Wii? Great, now I can show Tristan here how much of a cool dad I am by beating the two of you."

"You lost your coolness ages ago, when you decided to wear a Hawaiian shirt and flip flops with socks," I teased.

Tristan barked with laughter; I quickly joined him. It was Dad's turn to do an impression of a mock scowl.

The rest of the night played out with Tristan beating both my "apparently" cool father and myself at all the carnival games and all the sport games. It wasn't until later that night after saying a goodbye to Tristan and I was lying in bed that I realised I really enjoyed myself. Because of the company, and the fact that dad was home for a change. I asked him before heading to my room why he was home; he said he'd decided to take some time off, and he wanted to spend some time with me. That made tears spring to my eyes and I told him that sounded great. It was then he said that Tristan seemed like a nice young man, and he didn't think things between Sarah and Tristan would work. I asked him why, and he gave me a smirk and said Tristan was too smart for her. I rolled my eyes and continued on my way to my bedroom.

The time with Tristan also made me feel more comfortable about a friendship with him.

With time—I hoped those other deeper feelings I had for him would fade.

It could be possible if things kept going the way they were.

SIXTEEN

ALEXANDRA

Thursday at lunch, while Corbet was in the computer room, I told Sarah about Tristan coming over.

My hands were sweaty and I felt sick to my stomach, but I needn't have worried. She smiled and thought it was fantastic, and that it was really nice of my dad to ask him over. She also said it was great to hear that Tristan and I were getting along. Apparently, she'd been worried because I didn't like him, that it would cause problems between Tristan and herself. I managed a fake laugh and said that if I hadn't killed him last night, then it would be okay between us. And to my shock, she informed me that she wasn't sure now if things with Tristan were going to work out. He didn't want to sit with her at school; he didn't reply to her texts all the time, and she talked more to his friends than she did with him.

I couldn't believe my own ears and wanted to kick myself when I reassured her that they hadn't really gotten to know each other, and that she needed to give it time. She smiled and had said, "I can hope." And that was when I wanted to jump in front of a bus.

The conversation moved onto the upcoming weekend. Sarah wanted to do something different; she was sick of watching movie after movie. I supposed we had just about seen everything interesting at the video store. So I asked her what she had in mind; she then gave me a small, cunning smirk and said, "Leave it up to me."

At the time, I didn't think anything of it. I should have known though, by that look on her face, she was up to something. Friday came and went; Tristan couldn't make it to the library that night or Saturday because he'd had those two days off at the beginning of the, week and now they were swamped with extra work.

So Saturday came, and when Sarah turned up on my doorstep with Corbet, both of them looking like they were going out to a party, I started to panic. Sarah was dressed in tight black pants, a midriff pink top, and a black jacket. Her hair was flowing down around her shoulders, making her look like a runway model. Corbet was dressed in jeans and a white shirt, which looked really nice on him.

Alarm bells rang in my mind; they were way too overdressed for what I had been thinking we could do—like bowling, or mini golf.

What was going through Sarah's mind?

"Come on, Alex, let's get you changed and then we can be off." She stepped through the door and dragged me into my room.

"Whoa, where are we going exactly?" I asked, looking at Corbet because Sarah had disappeared into my walk-in wardrobe.

"Don't ask me; she won't tell," he said. Leaning in, he whispered, "But somehow I don't think we're going to like it."

"Funny, I have that feeling too," I admitted.

Sarah reappeared with an armful of clothing: dresses, skirts, tops, and jackets. I was sure it was all that I owned. She made me try on everything, until she was finally satisfied with a short floral dress and sandals.

"I will only wear this if I'm wearing leggings under it. Sarah, I haven't worn it for ages, and look how short it is now."

"Oh, all right party pooper, but let me tell you. You do have the legs to pull off that look, girl. I would ask Corbet if he didn't flee like he had." As soon as Sarah said 'try this on', Corbet ran for the door and down to the lounge to watch whatever my dad was.

I slipped on my black leggings under the dress and felt half-decent, and then much to Sarah's disgust, I grabbed a black jacket out and put it on.

"I'll freeze, especially if where we're going is outside."

"Nice try, trickster. You will just have to wait and see. But you and Corby have to keep an open mind, not run as soon as we step foot in there."

"That doesn't sound promising." If she already thought Corbet and I weren't going to like it, it was a probability that we wouldn't. But I knew Sarah, and she had an ulterior motive for taking us wherever it was we were going.

"Oh, stop it. Come on, let's get out of here."

I said my goodbye to Dad and asked him to wish me luck, saying that Sarah was the one to choose where we were heading without our knowledge of the destination. Dad being Dad was actually concerned, and I could see pity in his eyes as he wished me luck and warned Sarah to be nice and safe, or else. I gave him a quick hug and kiss, and he reminded me to not to be home too late and to be careful. To tell you the truth, I really would have preferred to stay home with Dad and watch some old funny movies. I even said that to him. But he said he was going to have an early night anyway because he wasn't feeling the best, and could be coming down with a cold.

As we pulled up out the front of Joe's, regret filled me. I shouldn't have agreed to this; I should be in my safe, warm house. I couldn't believe Sarah; this was asking way too much of me. It was safe to say that Corbet would have agreed with me by the pale, shocked look on his face as he got out of the car.

"No way. I am not going in there. Sarah, you know who hangs in there and how much shit they give not only one of your best friends, but the two of us."

"I know, but I made them promise to be on their best behaviour and they said they would be. They said that they'd love to get to know you guys like they have me."

Yes, I am sure that's what they want.

"Does Tristan know you're coming here, and with us?"

"No. I wanted to surprise him, but I told his friend Aaron about my idea of coming here to surprise him and that I wanted to bring you guys with me, and he thought it was a great idea."

It wasn't a great idea. Aaron was setting Sarah up, and I knew Tristan would also think it was a terrible idea. Yes, he wasn't going to like it one bit.

"Now, come on. Put on those brave faces for me and do this. Please, for me, and I promise I will never ask you guys to ever do anything you don't like again."

Corbet sighed and his shoulders dropped, but he nodded in agreement. Sarah then turned her pleading eyes to me.

"Stuff it, Sarah." I groaned. "This one time only, but if Corbet and I absolutely hate this place, we are leaving with or without you."

She cackled because she knew that we wouldn't leave without her, especially in a place like this.

Sarah squealed, grabbed our hands, and pulled us down the stairs into Joe's Pool Hall.

The door opened; the music hit us, and the smell of testosterone, sweat, smoke, and a tang of something else I couldn't put my finger on—and wasn't sure I really wanted to—filled our noses. Sarah dragged us over to the bar. This place did sell alcohol, but to get it, you had to have an ID on you.

I grabbed Sarah's hand tighter. She was glancing around to

see if she could find Tristan and his friends, while Corbet and I looked for the closest escape.

Joe's was huge for an underground place; there was at least twenty pool tables in the middle of the room, with low hanging lights over every table. Along all the other walls, besides the bar end, seated booths for those who only came here to watch and drink.

"There he is, and what the hell is that girl doing draped all over him?"

I looked over to the right corner, a few booths back from the bar, and found Tristan standing and leaning against the wall. His friends sat in the booth with some girls, but there was one girl with long brown hair, curled around Tristan. At least, he didn't look that interested in her, so I told that to Sarah while my eyes stayed glued to Tristan, and my heart did a double beat. He looked really good, leaning there in dark blue jeans and a tight black t-shirt.

"Yeah, well, he better not be. I'm going over; you guys coming?" She took a step forward, and then turned back to Corbet and me. However, we were quite comfortable where we were, having the bar helped us stand and not flee like I knew we wanted to.

"I think I might stay here and get a drink. Alex?"

"Yes, a drink sounds good, and then, you know how much of a shark playing pool-gal I am. I think I'm going to have a go at that. You up for it, Corbet?"

Corbet stifled his laugh and said, "Yeah, that sounds good; I bet I could beat your ass."

I raised my brows and snorted. "I highly doubt that."

Sarah scoffed, rolled her eyes, and left, but at least we brought a smile to her face. Corbet ordered us two cokes, and I watched Sarah arrive at the group. A few of Tristan's mates wolf-whistled at her. She ignored them and went straight up to Tristan and the girl. Sarah said something, the girl laughed and shook her head, then quickly left. Tristan seemed shocked for a second before he quickly recovered and smiled down at her. He said something, which made her point over our way, and I quickly looked to Corbet and said, "I think I would rather dye my hair pink than be here."

Corbet laughed. "I have to agree with you there, only I'd choose blue; pink is just not my colour, girlfriend."

I laughed and thought that the night just may be okay, if things could stay the way they were with Corbet and me joking around.

"Come on, let's head to a table and look like we know what we're doing," he said. I nodded and followed him over to a table on the left side of the room, farther away from Sarah. I liked his choice. He pulled out a few coins, placed them on the table, and then put one in the slot so the balls came out.

"I thought you didn't know what you're doing?" I asked, helping him place the balls on the table.

"I watch movies." He smiled. I laughed.

I wanted to look back over to Tristan, to see what they were doing, but I chose not to. I didn't want to catch his eye, so I kept my eyes on the game. Corbet had the first shot and got two smaller numbers in; he told me that the bigger numbers were the ones I had to aim for. So after he missed his next shot, I had a go, and to my surprise, I got one in. Not the one I was aiming for, but that didn't matter.

On our second game, after Corbet won the first, I took a chance and looked over after hearing laughter coming from that direction. Sarah was sitting down in the booth smiling away while Tristan was leaning over the side near her. He said something and they all cracked up laughing. I was glad to see her having a good time, but in a way, I kind of wished that was me. Then I felt guilty for even thinking it.

"I'm going to get another drink; this is thirsty work. Would you like one?" I said.

"Yeah, thanks." He didn't look up from his go, so I left him to it and made my way over to the bar. I had been so enthralled in the game that I hadn't noticed Joe's had gotten busier. I had to wait my turn to order a drink; it was a little crowded, but I finally found a spot at the bar. I quickly shoved in and waited again to get the bar guy's attention.

"Are you winning over there?" A voice next to me asked. I turned to my right to see a guy about two years older than me leaning against the bar, waiting for his turn to order a drink. He smiled down at me, like most people did because I was so short. He seemed like a nice guy; it helped he had a warm smile that made his blue eyes light up. It matched his sun-kissed hair and casual surfer look.

"No, not yet. My friend Corbet seems like he's enjoying himself, and when that happens, he gets competitive," I said.

"So he's just a friend?" he asked. I blushed and nodded.

We stood talking for a while. I found out his name was Simon Walker, and he was doing his apprenticeship to be a bricklayer. He liked to watch scary movies, listen to heavy metal rock, and wondered if he was doing the right job. He wanted to be in advertising, although he said he didn't have the brains for it. We laughed and talked, and I found myself really enjoying his company.

"Anyway, I had better get back over to Corbet. Thanks for the company." I smiled, grabbing the drink that'd been sitting there for a while. I hoped Corbet didn't mind it being a little warm and flat.

"Hang on," Simon called. I turned back around. "I was wondering if I could give you a kiss goodbye, something to remember me by." He smiled.

Now that was a line and I knew it, even though I'd never heard one before. I glanced over to Corbet, who was talking to Aaron; they didn't seem like they were arguing, and Corbet was laughing at something he was saying. Then I glanced over to Sarah and my stomach dropped; she was busy kissing Tristan as he leaned over the booth, while his friends looked on or at other things.

I looked back to Simon blushing. "I guess," I said. My heart rate picked up as he got closer. I moved my cheek closer to him, thinking that it would just be a quick cheek kiss because we hardly knew each other. I heard his laughter and blushed redder. He gently grabbed me under the chin and moved my face to look at his. His lips brushed mine and I gasped. I would never have done this, kiss a stranger in a public place, but a picture kept playing in my mind of Tristan kissing Sarah. So I pulled Simon closer, deepening the kiss. When his tongue made its way into my mouth, I could taste alcohol. I knew I should have stopped it then, but I didn't.

Then I was being pushed back. I opened my eyes to find Tristan standing in front of me, only I was looking at his back as he pushed Simon back even farther.

"Hold up, man, what's the problem?" Simon asked, holding up his hands in front of him to fend off Tristan.

"Leave her alone; she's mine," Tristan growled.

"Wait, she said nothing about having a boyfriend."

Oh, my God, who did Tristan think he was? I looked around to see where Sarah was; she was standing with Corbet and Aaron looking on, and she mouthed, "*Sorry.*"

Sorry? Sorry that Tristan was up here embarrassing me? Or sorry that she'd let him come up here?

I moved to stand next to Tristan, but he stepped in front of me again. Instead, I peered around him and said, "Simon, he's not...we're not..."

"If you're not her guy, who the hell do you think you are stopping her from having a good time?"

"I know you, Simon. You're here every weekend doing the same moves on unsuspecting girls."

Simon's whole expression changed. Instead of the nice smiling guy I was just kissing, he stood there with an arrogant smirk spread across his face. "Yeah, and so what? It's not like they don't enjoy it, and look at them— look at her." He gestured with his hand, only Tristan didn't move; he stood there facing

Simon with his arms crossed over his chest, feet spread apart. Seeming almost menacing. Still, Simon continued, "Who in the hell would play with that?" He laughed. "With glasses that frigging thick—, the body isn't bad, but those glasses. If anything, I was doing a service for the brotherhood." He laughed again.

Stuff it, what a jerk. He made me feel sick. I had just let him kiss me, touch me. I was disgusted at myself for letting that happen, but also for the fact that I had believed his words.

Who would want me?

Tristan pulled his arm back as though he was going to hit Simon. I quickly grabbed hold of it, and he looked down at me. Whatever he saw stopped him; instead, he faced me with his whole body, blocking out Simon.

"He's not worth it," I uttered. *I am not worth it.*

He searched my face for an answer, and in the end, he nodded. For a second, I thought he was going to step forward and hug me, but my phone rang. I dug around in my bag until I found it, pulled it free, and quickly answered it before whoever it was hung up.

"Hello?" I said.

"Is this, Alexandra Harmony?" asked a light female voice.

"Yes it is."

"I am sorry to inform you, but your father has been in an accident. You need to come to the Base Hospital right away."

I froze. My mind wouldn't— no, *couldn't* comprehend those words.

"Alex, what is it?" Tristan asked. He waved behind me to someone.

"Miss. Miss, are you there?"

"I…uh, yes, yes I'm here."

"Your father is being operated on now; you need to come here."

"Okay, all right. I'll be there." I pulled the phone away from my ear and hung it up, but looked at it. Just looked at it.

Had that been real?

"Alex, babe, who was that?" Sarah asked from beside me. I glanced at her and saw that Corbet was next to her, then back at my phone. I looked up to Tristan's concerned face, and next to him was Aaron, who seemed confused. "She's in shock. Someone slap her," Sarah suggested.

"I will," Aaron offered.

"You won't touch her," Tristan growled. God, he could sound so tough, so scary when he wanted to be. "Damn it, Alex, snap out of it; what's going on?" he barked, getting all up in my face.

"What? Oh, oh God—I have to get to the Base Hospital, m —my dad...he's been in an accident of some kind, th—they didn't tell me what, but what can it be? He said he was going to stay home tonight. Oh, maybe he fell over in the house. That's just a small accident, isn't it? He's going to be fine, right? But I have to go. I have to go, now."

"Right." Tristan nodded. "Alex, get your ass up those stairs. Corbet take Sarah home. Aaron, I'm taking your car; give me your keys."

I heard keys being shuffled around, and Sarah grabbed me into her arms and whispered, "Everything will be all right, and your dad's going to be fine. It's all right—okay, Alex, your dad's all good. Don't worry about *anything*," she comforted.

I didn't get to ask what she meant about the last 'anything' part because Corbet's arms tangled around me in an awkward hug. "Don't stress, pet. He's strong; he'll be fine." He stepped back and said with a slap on my butt, "Now get going." Then to someone behind me, "Sorry, man." He held up his hands, waving them. Next thing I knew, someone had a hand on my waist and I was being forced out of Joe's and into the cool night air. I was gently forced through the car park next to Joe's and to a busted-up, dark red car. The passenger's door opened, someone helped me in, and to my surprise, the car actually started.

"Alex." I looked to the person next to me and found Tristan looking back worriedly.

"Yes?"

"Are you okay? Stupid question, but you're worrying me; say something, please," he asked as he pulled out of the car park.

My bottom lip trembled. "I can't lose him, Tristan, not him too," I said and then burst into tears. Tristan reached over, taking my hand in his. He brought it to his chest, trying to give me reassuring words, but right then, nothing was helping. Nothing would, not until I saw him for myself and found out he was okay and what had happened.

I had to let myself feel the emotions and cry until I got to the hospital. I could allow myself to sob like I was, even if I'd be embarrassed by it later for doing it in front of Tristan. But once we got there, I would stop; I would have myself under control. I needed to for my dad. Like my dad was strong for me, when Mom…when she passed away.

PART
THREE

SEVENTEEN

SKYLAR

I stood out in front of Kane's house in the driveway like a stunned deer. I didn't know which way to go or if the buses were still running. I knew I didn't have enough money for the taxi to take me all the way to the Base Hospital.

I let out a frustrated scream; all I wanted to do was get there to see my Momma, to make sure she was all right, and then yell at her for putting herself in danger.

My hands hurt, so I looked down at them; they were clenched tightly into balls. I stomped my feet, getting more annoyed with myself.

Just move, girl. Just move; get there one way or another.

I picked up my dress once more and started for the end of the driveway; once there, I stopped short, eyes wide. There was Kane, sitting in a Hummer with the passenger's door open.

How did he get there so fast?

Because you wasted time standing in the driveway.

"What—"

"Come on, Sky, get in."

I quickly jumped in and shut the door with no other thought than this would get me there faster than what I'd had in mind. Kane started to drive off, and I was sure that he was going over the speed limit.

"Shouldn't you be back there with Donna?" I asked acidly. I couldn't help it. Anger was overriding me. If I let go, I'd be no good to Momma or myself. "Just give me the car and you can go back."

"No."

"What, you don't trust me with this precious vehicle, or is it you're worried what Mommy, dearest thinks? Because we both know she doesn't like me. Damn it, Kane, just pull over; go back to your happy life. I promise I won't disappear on Dommy; I couldn't do that to her, but I need you to go back to Donna. You know she'll make it worth your while."

Did he need me to scream it? I didn't want him here, near me.

"You finished?" he quietly asked while not taking his eyes off the road.

When I didn't answer, he took that as a yes and said, "I'm sorry you heard what you did, and I know you're angry. But you are stuck with me through this, whether you like it or not."

"I don't want you." Here, there, or anywhere—never.

"It doesn't matter," he uttered, then reached over and took my hand in his, resting them on my thigh. I didn't push him away. I should have, but I couldn't.

The rest of the drive was silent. Kane pulled up front of the hospital, not bothering with the car park area. I dove out, and so did Kane; he came around to my side, grabbed my hand, and together we ran inside, straight up to the front desk.

"I need...I—I have to see Jenny James."

"Sky." I turned to find Barbra getting up from a waiting room chair. She looked defeated, absolutely drained.

"Barb, please tell me she's okay, please. If anything has happened, I can't...it's...No! I'll—I'll find this jerk that shot her and shoot him myself," I yelled. Barbra came over quickly, pulling me into a hug.

"She's okay; she's pulled through. Only they're keeping her asleep until morning, for the shock and pain." I nodded into her shoulder.

Thank you, God, thank you for taking care of her.

I still wanted to see her. I left Kane out with Barbra and went through a passageway, down a hall, and into her room.

And that was all I needed. I just needed to see her, even if she had tubes sticking out of her arms. I just needed to see with my own eyes that she was still breathing. I took a hold of her hand and then kissed her forehead.

"I love you, Momma. Don't you ever scare me like this again," I scolded with a whisper into her ear. I wiped away the one tear that dared to come out. "I'll see you right here in the morning, so don't go getting any other ideas. Night, Momma." I kissed her one last time and walked out of the room.

Kane looked up as the doors opened. He was sitting with Barbra on those uncomfortable, cold-looking, plastic waiting chairs. He didn't seemed too scared or worried, so Barbra couldn't have pestered him with too many bad questions. Not that this was the time. Still, no one could know what would come out of Barbra most of the time.

"You all right, hon?"

I nodded and smiled up at her. "I just needed to see her for myself."

"Of course you did."

"How did it happen, Barb? Did they catch the guy?"

She sighed loudly, rolled her neck, and then rubbed at it. "Some dipshit came in with a gun, and your Momma was the first register he saw and went to. She was being her stubborn idiotic self and said no when he asked for her money. Her customer at the time told her to hand it over, but still she didn't. He got pissed and shot her. Her customer tried to jump in front of her, protect her, I guess, but he was shot too."

I actually did a girly gasp. "Is he okay? Is he here?"

"As far as I know, he is. His daughter is in with him now. That's her guy over there, I think; well, he came in with her." I looked over to a hulking figure of a guy, dressed in blue jeans and a black tee. His eyes were a dark green and looked like they could pierce you on the spot, and his hair was jet black. He gave me a small chin lift that I quickly returned. Kane came closer. I could feel him at my right side, his warmth invading my personal space. It felt great.

"Go on, hon, get home and rest. I know you'll be here at the crack of dawn. I only stayed to see you, but now that I know you have your beau with you, I don't need to worry. It was nice meeting you, Kane."

"You too, Mrs Keating."

I didn't bother informing her of her mistake when she called Kane my beau; instead, I gave her one last hug and watched her leave.

A hand touched my waist; I jumped, and the hand left. "You ready to leave?" Kane asked.

I stared at the doors closing after Barb had left. "I know I should, but...I don't know. I just feel like I should be doing something."

"I can't say I understand what you mean—what you're going through right now—because I really hate it when people say 'I understand' when really they don't. So all I can say is that when you're ready, we'll go. And, Sky...I am here for you."

Was he concerned because I hadn't cried yet? Did he think I'd go mad or something?

He didn't need to worry. I'd be doing that later, when my brain stopped thinking and I was alone.

I didn't know what to say to him, so all I said was, "Come on."

We walked out, side-by-side. I really did want to reach out to him, and fold myself into his heat, into his arms. Still, I didn't.

Once outside, we moved to the car that was still waiting near the doors. Kane walked around the front and got in the already-opened door.

"Didn't you lock it?" I asked, dumbfounded.

He gave me a small smiled. "No, and apparently I left the keys in it as well." With a small laugh, he lifted the keys out of the ignition. I shook my head at him and laughed too.

"How could you have done that, Kane? Someone could have stolen it."

He looked to the front of the car, shrugged, and stared back at me, mildly saying, "I didn't want you to go in alone, and I knew you wouldn't wait for me. The car didn't cross my mind."

I had to say something, how nice that was. Hell, he left his car to be stolen and ran after me.

Would he have done it for Donna?

Just that one thought dried up the compassion I was feeling for Kane. I nodded and went to climb into the car, but stopped. I was halfway up, but quickly got back out and took some steps towards the hospital doors.

"Sky, what is it?" Kane asked. I didn't know, though—a feeling? A thought? "Sky?" I heard his door slam; I knew he was coming around the car to me, then I felt and smelt his jacket being place on my shoulders, and I quickly put my arms through the sleeves.

"I—I don't know. Kane, I feel like I should be doing something."

"Sky, there's nothing more you can do," he said with concern in his voice. He placed his hand on my waist and when I didn't flinch he tried to move me to the car.

"No wait," I said. I looked to the doors of the hospital. That guy I'd seen in there was coming out, and in front of him was a short girl wearing glasses, a floral dress, leggings, and a black jacket. I felt myself moving towards her quickly as she moved to me.

I came to a stop in front of her, my head tilted to the side and I stared at her, just like she was at me. "It was your dad who tried to save my Momma?" She nodded. Maybe this was why I felt I had to meet her, see her?

I held out my hand. "I'm Skylar."

She smiled and said, "I'm Alexandra."

EIGHTEEN

ALEXANDRA

The drive felt long, and I cried the whole way. Tristan tried to give me more reassuring words, but when I wouldn't stop, he left me to cry, still holding my hand in his. When we pulled up into the hospital car park, I drew in a deep breath and got myself together. I went to reach for my bag, but it wasn't on the floor in front of me.

"Tristan, I forgot my bag. Stuff it; I left it back at Joe's."

He seemed a little shocked by my surprise recovery, but I knew I had to. "It's in the back; Sarah gave it to me."

I blushed, reached over, pulled out some tissues, and blew my nose. Charming, I know, but it is better than having snot running down my face. I cleared my voice, "Thanks for the lift. I'm sorry I was such a mess. You…ah, can get back to Sarah now. I don't know how long I'm going to be in there, and I really have to go, so thanks again." I undid the seat belt and got out of the car.

I walked around the car, head hanging low while I made sure I had everything in my bag and trying to distract my thoughts. I picked up speed, need hitting me to get in there, to find out answers.

I was near the sliding doors, looking at the black Hummer left out the front with its keys in it. Someone was sure in a hurry, like I should be.

I went to walk around it when someone placed their hand in mine. I turned too quickly, causing me to lose my footing, but thankfully, Tristan was there to place his hand around my waist and straighten me back up, into his arms.

For a second, all I wanted to do was stand there with my forehead leaning against his chest and think of nothing else. I was more than reluctant to go in there in case it was bad news waiting for me.

Still, now was the time to be brave.

"What are you doing?" I asked. I hadn't heard him approach, or even when he got out of the car.

"You are not doing this on your own. Come on." He moved his hands from around my waist and placed it in mine, leading me into the hospital.

We walked up to the counter where the nurse was flirting with the security guy. She was laughing, and that made me feel angry. The security guy gave us a once over and stepped back, but I noticed he didn't take his eyes off Tristan, who was nearly double his size.

"I'm—my dad, he—someone called me," I stuttered out.

Concern showed in her eyes. "That was me, dear. He's out of surgery and it looks like he's going to be okay. They're keeping him unconscious until morning."

"What...uh, what happened?"

"All I know is that he was at the supermarket when a man came in to rob it. When he didn't get the money, he went to shoot the cashier, and your dad jumped in front of her. But they both ended up being shot then."

No, no. He was shot, shot by a real gun! How can one do such a thing? And what was he thinking?

"Alexandra, are you okay?" Tristan asked. I looked up at him and nodded. "He's going to be okay." He smiled, and I nodded again. "Can she see him?" Tristan asked what I was thinking.

The security guy coughed and said, "No visitors now; he's asleep anyway 'til morning."

"So at least let her see him, so she can reassure herself that he is okay." Tristan glared.

"Look, mate, rules are rules," he said, standing up taller and placing his hands on his belt—one on his Taser gun.

"Come on, you let Sky through to see her mom," a voice said behind me. I looked over my shoulder to find a guy about my age standing there—in a tuxedo, of all things—with an older lady.

"It's all right, Mack, let the girl through. We're so slow tonight; the other nurses haven't come back from break," the nurse said then grumbled under her breath, "Wenches, just wait till I go on my break. Knowing my luck, we'll have more patients come in and I'll have to come back."

The security guy grumbled, but opened the door anyway. I said a thank you to the tuxedo guy and went to walk through the door, but stopped and looked back over to Tristan.

"I'll be here when you come out," he said. I gave him a small smile and kept going. The hospital, for once, seemed dead quiet, which was really creepy because from what I had heard, hospitals were usually busy at night because of drunks, drug users, and people in fights.

I was told where his room was, and the walk down the hall seemed long. I opened the door to room 424 and gasped at the sight of my dad hooked up to so many machines.

As I took the few steps to his bedside, I fought back the tears wanting to escape.

"Dad? Oh, Daddy, I love you. Please don't ever scare me like this again. I can't lose you too. I don't know what I would do if I did. And what in God's name were you doing at the grocery store so late at night?"

I giggled, bent, and kissed him on the cheek. "She must have been good-looking for you to want to risk your life. I'll see you in the morning; be a good man and stay safe. Love you." I gave him one last hand squeeze and kiss on the cheek, then left.

I went back down the hall, wanting to ask the nurse some questions. The security guy must have seen me approaching because the door opened, and I walked back out into the quiet waiting room. A room that had always made me uncomfortable. At least this wasn't the hospital I had lost my mother in, because if it was, I honestly didn't think I would have been able to set one foot in here.

Tristan stood up as I came out; I gave him a reassuring smile as he walked over to me.

"Are you okay?"

"Better. Thank you for...for being here, helping me get to see him. I don't think I would have calmed down if I hadn't."

"I figured that, and I have to say, you look better now that you have seen him. Before, you were ghostly white."

"I just want to ask a few questions and then we can go. If you could just drop me off at home, then you can get back to Sarah. I wonder if she's still..." My voice travelled off because I had a sudden urge to go outside.

"Alex? Alexandra, what is it?" Tristan caught my arm. I hadn't realised I had already started to walk off until I was no longer standing in front of him. "Alex?"

"I...I don't know, Tristan. Just..."

"Alex, didn't you want to ask some questions?"

I looked back at him and then to the door again; through them, I could see a girl in a long black dress and her hair pulled up, and the same guy I had seen before in a tuxedo. I shook my head and looked back at Tristan's worried expression. "Yes, yes, I do have questions. But...wait one minute." This time, he let go and followed me out the front doors.

I was walking down the front path; the girl was heading right for me, with tuxedo guy behind her. Where had they come from to be dressed like that?

My head went to the side, trying to figure out what I was feeling inside of myself, but then she spoke, "It was your dad who tried to save my Momma."

I nodded; she held out her hand to me, "I'm Skylar."

I smiled at her. "I'm Alexandra."

NINETEEN

SKYLAR

"I'm sorry about your dad," I said, not knowing what else to say.

She nodded. "And I'm sorry about your mom. Is she going to be okay?" she asked with true concern showing in her eyes.

"Yeah. And your dad?"

"Yes. He's going to be fine." She smiled.

I grinned. "I guess they'll both be getting a serious talk from the both of us tomorrow."

Alexandra giggled. "Yes, that will be in the cards."

Shivering when the wind picked up, I hugged Kane's jacket tighter.

Kane stepped forward and placed his hand on the small of my back. "We better get going."

Nodding, I met Alexandra's eyes once again. "I'll probably see you tomorrow, right?"

"I'll be here as soon as visiting hours start," she said, and pushed her glasses higher on her nose. I couldn't help but smile. She seemed like a nerd, but somehow I knew our lives would be joined from this night on, and I was looking forward to getting to know her.

I gave a chin lift to her fella, a quick hug to Alexandra, and whispered in her ear, "Are you going to be okay tonight?"

"I think so...and you?"

Pulling back, I grinned. "Yeah. See you tomorrow."

"Till then."

Yep. Nerd. But in a cute way.

Kane took my hand and led me back to the car. Once I was in, he closed the door, and quickly went around and jumped in. We drove silently to my house while I fought back the emotions that wanted out.

My momma was going to be okay. That was all I had to think of.

Kane stopped the car in my driveway. I got out and realised then that I didn't have my keys. Thank God, for the spare key Momma had hidden under the front door mat.

"You need a better hiding place," Kane said. I jumped because I thought he was still in the car and was going to drive away...back to Donna.

"What are you doing? You should go. I'm fine; you've done your knightly duty." I needed time alone to cry the shock and fright from the night out of my system.

I turned back to the door and went to unlock it, but my hands shook so much it made it hard. Kane leaned over, placed his hand on mine to steady it, and unlocked the door.

"I'm not leaving, Skylar." His whisper sent a shiver down my spine.

But he had to leave.

There was no way I was going to cry in front of him.

I didn't move to enter the house. Looking down at the mat at the front door, I uttered, "You have to. Donna's waiting."

"I don't care."

Why?

With a hand at the small of my back, he gently pushed me forward into the house. I turned on the light and made my way to the kitchen, busying myself with putting on the kettle for a coffee. When I reached up into the cupboard to grab the mugs, I felt him walk up behind me. He put his hands on my waist.

My movement paused for a second, and then I placed the mugs on the bench. "What are you doing, Kane?" I whispered to the bench.

"It's okay to let it out, Sky," he said, with his chin on my shoulder and his hands *still* at my waist.

"No." I shook my head.

"Sky."

I shook my head again. "No. No, Kane, you have to leave. Just leave me alone."

"Never gonna happen."

A sob caught in my throat. "You have to."

"No."

He turned me in his arms and wrapped them around my waist tightly, bringing me to the front of his body. I tried to push him away, but he wouldn't have it.

"It's okay, baby."

My struggling stopped at his words. I gripped his shirt and broke the dam down. I cried for nearly losing my momma. For the thought of being left alone if anything had happened to her. For the pain she must have felt. For the hurt that sliced through me with that one phone call. For seeing my brave, strong Momma lying silently after being through hell.

I also cried for something I would never have. Kane.

After some time, Kane picked me up in his arms and carried me to my bedroom. He laid me out on my bed and left, but only to come back seconds later.

"I've turned everything off and locked up," he said.

I mumbled a thanks through my crying. Seconds later, I felt the bed shift behind me.

"Scoot over. It's not really big enough for the two of us, but we'll make it work."

When I didn't move and he realised I wasn't going to, he somehow moved me across, flipped me over, and cradled me to his body.

"You're even stubborn when you're like this. Unbelievable,"

he muttered to the top of my head, where it was resting against his chest.

I wasn't the stubborn one. I wasn't the one who wouldn't leave when someone had repeatedly asked them to. Even though I was more than grateful for having him here—something I would never tell him. I placed my arms around his waist and pulled him closer to me. I fell asleep, once I was all cried out.

TWENTY

ALEXANDRA

On the drive home, I kept thinking of ways to show Tristan my appreciation. He didn't have to come—Corbet or Sarah could have taken me—but he took control of the whole situation. Maybe I could cook for him one night? I could offer to do his homework for a week. Still, I felt nothing would be enough. I also doubted he would want me to do anything for him in return for taking care of me when I needed it.

"Alexandra?" Tristan said.

"Hmm?"

He chuckled. "We're here." He unbuckled his seat belt and climbed out of the car. Before he had a chance to come around my side, I quickly got out.

I walked up to the front door, unlocked it, and then turned on the lounge light. Without stopping, I made my way into the kitchen. To do what, I wasn't sure.

I stopped at the kitchen bench and gripped it.

My dad was going to be okay.

That was good.

No, that was more than good.

I felt that I should have been crying, but I'd done enough on the way to the hospital, and now the relief of knowing that he was going to be fine overrode anything.

I felt happy.

Exhausted, but content.

"Alexandra?"

"Hmm?"

This felt familiar.

Another chuckle. "I think it'd be good if you got some sleep."

"Hmm."

His heat hit my back. I felt his hands at my shoulders, turning me and gently ushering me out of the kitchen, down the hall, and up the stairs to my room. We stopped at the threshold.

"Tristan," I said.

"Yeah, baby?"

Oh, my. That sounded good.

"T—thank you," I stuttered. He wrapped his arms around my chest and brought my back flush with his front. "I—I want to thank you for *everything* you've done for me tonight."

"You don't need to. I'm glad I was there."

I nodded.

"Baby, go and get ready for bed. You must be tired."

"Yes."

His lips touched my neck, right near my shoulder. Before I could react, he gently shoved me forward.

"I'll go turn everything off."

Turning, I called, "Tristan."

He poked his head around the corner. "Yeah?"

"A—are you going? I mean, is Sarah waiting for you? Or Aaron, for his car?"

"Nah, none of the above. I'll be back in a second," he said and disappeared.

I quickly got out of my clothes and into my pyjamas, which consisted of guy boxers and tee. My heart was in overdrive.

He was coming back.

Here in my room?

With me?

Pulling back my covers of my queen bed, I climbed in and brought the covers up to my chin.

Tristan walked in seconds later, and without looking at me, he pulled his tee over his head in one smooth move. He had his jeans off in the next second, and I had another moment to admire his body before he flung back the covers and climbed in.

He rolled to his side facing me, and said, "The house is all locked up and everything is turned off. Time for some sleep, babe."

As I lay on my back with my head turned towards him, I thought how lucky I was to have him as a friend. What also crossed my mind was how the temperature in the room seemed to be at a boiling point. Or it could have had something to do with the fact that Tristan was in my bed.

With me.

"You all right?" Tristan asked.

"Mm-hm."

I was all right. I was more than all right. My dad was healing; he was going to get better.

The covers were moving. They were tugged from my tight grip and Tristan lifted them and moved closer to me. His arm wrapped around my waist, and he moved me so I was facing the window and he was at my back, hugging me to him.

It was so sweet that it made me want to cry.

I think my stupid crush just escalated to a full-blown one.

Deep, heart-wrenching feelings flew through my veins.

"Alexandra?"

"Hmm?"

He chuckled. "Babe, do you usually sleep with your glasses on?"

I was such a nerd.

"No," I said, but made no move to remove them. I was way too warm, comfortable, and content.

"I can see in these types of situations you turn into a zombie." He laughed. His breath fanned the back of my neck. He reached over and slowly took my glasses from my face. I felt him roll onto his back and heard him place them onto my bedside table. The bed dipped as he rolled back and brought me tightly against him once again with his arm around my waist.

"Tristan?" I whispered to the room.

"Yeah?"

"Thank you for staying. You can be really sweet...um, I mean, ah...nice."

He said nothing, but I didn't miss that he tensed at my words. Had I said the wrong thing? I was only telling him what I felt...so maybe that was wrong.

I was near sleep-land when I heard his reply, "No, I'm anything but nice."

TWENTY-ONE

SKYLAR

Warmth from another body was something that had never woken me before. I opened my eyes and had a semi-freak out. I knew it was Kane, but having him there, in my bed with me, and everything he'd seen last night made my already wild emotions go crazier. I wanted to roll over and attack him. I wanted to kiss, lick, hug, and touch him in every way. I wanted to cry, smile, sing, and scream how happy he made my heart feel.

He wasn't like all the others...he was different; he was special.

But he also wasn't for me.

And he never would be.

We were too different. His mother would never accept someone like me in his life, and I would never want to come between Kane and his family.

Even if she was a bitch with a capital B.

That was his life. He was used to money. He'd never have to struggle in life, and I knew that being with me, his life would be full of struggle, full of regret, and I could never do that to him.

He needed to go back to Donna...that was, if they were actually still broken up.

He shifted behind me and rubbed the front of his body to my back.

Did he think I was Donna?

I needed to get up, but I knew this was the only chance I would get having Kane this close to me again, and I wanted to cherish it a little longer.

"Morning," he whispered behind me, and then got up on his elbow to look at me over my shoulder. His smile was pure magic.

I wanted to cry.

"H—hey." My voice broke.

"You okay?"

I shrugged. He moved my hair gently over my shoulder, sending tingles down my back.

"I need to get up," I said, and flung the cover from my body. I went to get out of bed, until his arm wound around my waist and pulled me back against him. But apparently, that wasn't enough; he moved me so I was lying on my back and he was looking down at me with a concerned expression upon his face, his brows drawn together.

"Skylar…"

"I—I have to get to the hospital."

"I'll take you in a minute."

"No. I'll take a bus; you should get home." *To Donna.*

He closed his eyes and when he opened them, all I saw was warmth and humour. "Don't close me out," he whispered. "I know you're probably freaked about a lot of things…but don't close me out, please."

It was my turn to close my eyes, so I could block out his kind words and the tears that threatened to break free; only to open them wide in shock when I felt his lips upon mine.

Holy heck.

I wasn't strong enough for this. I wasn't strong enough to push him away.

One time wouldn't hurt…right?

I wrapped my arms around his neck and brought him closer. He took the hint and deepened the kiss; our tongues fought for control.

His hand threaded through my hair, tightly gripping it, causing me to moan against his mouth. That must have urged him on because his hand left my hair and went down to my waist to slip up the tee I was wearing. I'd put it on during the night because I was no longer comfortable in the dress I had been wearing.

His finger gently stroked my stomach, causing butterflies to take flight. My own hands left his neck and made their way down his back to slip under his shirt.

I woke out of my kissing slumber when I felt his finger trace under my boob. I broke free from the kiss and pushed against his chest.

"No."

"Shit. Sorry. God, I'm sorry." He rested his forehead against mine. "I seem to get carried away where you're concerned." He smiled.

I pushed against his chest again and he moved back to look down at me. "I…" Hell, this was going to hurt me, but it had to be done. I glared up at him. "Just because you didn't get what you wanted from Donna last night, doesn't mean I'm the easy target, just 'cause I'm all messed up right now."

"Sky, I would never—"

"Save it for your girlfriend. Move. I need to get showered and changed."

He smiled, and then he started chuckling. Which pissed me off.

"Move," I snapped.

"No. I see what you're doing. Giving me your attitude when things start getting too much for you. But it won't work. Yes, I shouldn't have…well, you know. Still, it had nothing to do with Donna and what she offered me last night. Because honestly, she was far from my mind, and has been since I sat down at our history desk. You are the one who consumes my thoughts these days." He ran his finger gently over my cheek.

"Don't. Don't do this; you're not thinking straight. Things got carried away and now you're thinking with what's down there." I gestured with my eyes to his lower half. "When things settle down, you'll regret everything you've just said. This...us, won't work. I don't want it to. I never think of you. I don't want you."

He laughed. I punched his chest.

"All right, babe. I see this was too soon and too much for you to handle right now. But let me tell you, before I let you crawl back into your hard shell, that I know when you're lying. You want this. *You* want *me*, and no matter how much you fight, I'll keep coming back for more until I wear you down."

My heart exploded. That was the only excuse I had for staring at him, flabbergasted. I had never known Kane to be this...sure of himself before.

He chuckled. "I can see I've shocked you, so we'll leave things...for now." He pecked me on the lips and rolled away, placing his hand behind his head and smiling like he just won the lottery.

"Get a move on, Sky. I've got to drop you off, go home, shower, and come pick you up again."

I shook my head to clear it. Did he really say everything he just said?

"Um, no. I mean, you can't pick me up. Um, Jessie said she was." I needed time away from him to gain back my sanity.

"Really? And when did you organise this?" He smiled.

Damn.

"Ah..." I sat up and placed my feet on the floor. Taking a deep breath, I said, "Kane, I—I just...please, let me just have some time."

"So you can convince with yourself that this isn't right? No."

I stood, turned, and glared down at him with my hands on my hips. "Kane. I don't need this right now. My momma was shot last night; all my thoughts are wrapped tightly around her, and then you just dump all this shit on me right now? When all I want is to hurry and go to the hospital to see her. Do you think this is fair? You need to get it through your thick head that we are never going to happen. You still have a girlfriend for God's sake," I shouted.

He was in front of me in a second, his hands at my waist, and pulled me forward so we were toe-to-toe. "My timing does suck; I'll give you that. But I want you to understand that I do *not* have a girlfriend. And no, this wasn't fair to drop all this on you right now...so I'll wait. I know you'll have more defences up, but I'll knock them down, and any excuse you give me won't be enough. This...us...is happening. Now, go shower, babe." With that, he kissed me on my nose, turned me, and gently shoved me forward. My body did the rest; it grabbed clothes and went off to the bathroom for a shower.

My mind was still spinning from this new Kane and the way he was making me feel.

I was in deep doo-doo.

TWENTY-TWO

ALEXANDRA

All of a sudden, it was hard to breath. There was a heavy weight on top of me and I needed it off. I opened my eyes and found what that weight was...Tristan.

He had his left side on the bed, but the rest of him was over the top of me. His arm and leg were flung over my chest and both of my legs. His head was rested upon my shoulder, snuggled up to my face, and for the life of me, even though it was hard to breath, I didn't have the heart to wake him. He looked so peaceful; usually his brooding attitude and the permanent scowl showed people that he wasn't to be messed with. But the way his face was relaxed then, he looked like a big, soft, cute, nice teddy bear.

Not that I would ever tell him that.

He started to move. I panicked and closed my eyes, faking sleep. I felt him stretch, and then he stilled when he figured out someone else was in bed. His heat left me; the bed dipped enough that I knew he'd sat up, and then I heard his feet hit the floor.

"Shit," he whispered. My heart clenched. "What the hell was I thinkin'?"

Hurt sliced through me. Tears welled behind my closed eyes.

He was disgusted because he woke up beside the school's nerd. A tear escaped. I rolled to my side away from him so he wouldn't witness the pain that cut deep in my heart and stomach.

I couldn't blame him for thinking anything bad. I knew I was nothing to look at, and I also knew Tristan was way out of my league.

What was he thinking?

And what was I thinking when he was being so nice to me, helping me through last night? I should have known that it would never change the situation between us.

I should have known.

I had no one else to blame for the pain I was feeling but myself.

With minimal movement, I wiped the tears away. I had to fix this…but how?

Rolling over, I opened my eyes. They landed on Tristan, who was sitting on the side of the bed, but his eyes were on me.

"Morning." I smiled. It nearly faltered, but I forced it to stay in place.

"Hey…look, I have to go. I gotta take Aaron's car back."

I nodded. "Okay."

"Listen, ah, nothing's changed between us, so don't get any ideas we're together now or anything." He laughed.

"I know…I mean…I won't." I sat up and pulled the blankets up my body, trying to keep the heat in, but his words and the frustrated look upon his face made me feel cold to the bone.

"Good. 'Cause you aren't exactly my type; I'd never go for someone like you."

My eyes closed. I took a deep breath and opened them to glare at him. "I get it, Tristan. Boy, do I get it. You don't need to be an ass about it."

He looked down between his feet to the floor. "See, I do, because that's what I am." Shaking his head, he looked back at me with a sneer. "We're done with the tutoring crap. I'll work it out from here. I don't need your help."

Clenching my fist didn't help me fight the tears; some escaped. He saw them, and for a second he seemed regretful, but it soon changed to a scowl.

"Thank you, Tristan, for telling me how it is. But do you know what? You really didn't need to. I already knew you were mortified to have my help in the first place, and even more so if someone caught us together. I'm the nerd, the short, thick glasses-wearing loser. You're...well, you're you." I gestured at him with my hand. "But again, thank you for setting me straight with something I already knew, and especially for doing it today, after the night I just had." I flung the covers back, got out of bed, and stalked to the door. "I still want to thank you for...last night." My voice broke.

I cleared it and continued, "Now, I'm going for a shower. I expect you'll be gone before I get out." I looked away from him, out into the hall. "You're right, Tristan...what the hell were you thinking?" With that, I walked out, down the hall, and into the bathroom. Once I had the door closed, I leaned against it, my breathing laboured. My hand went to my chest as the first sob escaped. I slid down the wall onto the floor and broke down.

I cried for caring, for his hurtful words, the look upon his face that wouldn't disappear from my mind.

Only I didn't let myself cry for long. I felt stupid for crying in the first place, when I should have known all along that it would turn out this way. He was just like the others...but in a way so much worse.

TWENTY-THREE

SKYLAR

After I showered and got dressed, I found Kane in the kitchen. He'd made me some toast, which I took and ate on the way to the hospital. We pulled up out the front. He turned to me and grabbed my wrist before I could make a quick escape.

"I'm sure you'll ring Jessie to come and get you after here, so I'll let you."

I snorted. He'd *let* me?

"I know you need time to take in what I've said to you, so I'll give it to you, but remember that no matter how much you'll fight against what's going to happen between us, I'll be ready to fight back." He leaned closer and whispered, "And I'll win." His fingers went into my hair and he pulled me forward; our lips touched with a quick rough kiss. "Looking forward to it, babe." He let go, and I staggered from the car and into the hospital, dazed and confused.

I shook my head and smiled to myself, because what Kane didn't realize was that I also liked to fight, and I didn't like to lose.

It was never going to happen between us. For his sake, in the long run, I would never let it happen. I just couldn't for the life of me understand the sudden change in Kane.

"Skylar?" I heard a quiet voice call.

Turning, I came face-to-face with Alexandra.

"Hi." I smiled, but it faded once I took in her red eyes and sad expression. "What's happened? Are they okay?"

"What? Oh, oh yes, our parents are fine. I just asked the nurse. I'm working my way to go in there; I just don't want Dad to think I'm a mess because of him."

"Then why…"

"Why am I a mess? Another reason." She smiled sadly and looked out the front doors.

"That guy from last night?"

Still not meeting my gaze, she nodded and bit her bottom lip.

"Do I need to beat the guy up?"

She giggled. "No. But thank you. It's just me being silly."

"Wanna talk about it?"

She smiled, her eyes warming. "Maybe later…and maybe you could tell me why you walked in here looking so…"

"Freaked?" I offered. Because I was freaked in a big way.

"Yes." She laughed.

"Sure. I'd like that."

"Great. After we see our parents, we could go somewhere for a coffee or something."

"That'd be great. Would you mind if I asked my friend along? You'll like her, and then I won't have to repeat it to her later."

Her brows furrowed. "That's fine."

"Are you sure?"

She shook her head. "Sorry, yes, I'm sure. I was just…don't worry; I'll tell you later."

I grinned. "Deal." I turned to walk alongside her, knowing our parents were on the same small floor and hallway.

"When I spoke to the nurse earlier, she informed me that our parents have been moved to the second floor and into the same room."

"That's good then. At least I'll get to thank your dad at the same time as I tell my Momma off."

TWENTY-FOUR

ALEXANDRA

The door to the room was closed; we knocked, and a female called for us to enter. Skylar opened the door and walked in first. I spotted her mom in the first bed closest to the door, and she had tears shining in her eyes seeing it was Skylar. She held open her arms and Skylar dove into them.

"Oh, my baby girl. I am so sorry to scare you."

"You will *never* do it again," Skylar scolded.

I looked over to the far bed and found Dad sitting up in bed smiling at me, our own eyes glistening with tears. I was across the room in seconds and in his arms, being careful of the wound in his shoulder.

"Dad, you are *not* to go out to the supermarket again on your own."

"I know, sweetheart. I can't believe I nearly left you."

More tears came, and I held back a sob. "I can't lose you too Dad, never. You have to be safe."

"I will, princess. I will be."

"Don't worry, Alex. If I know my Momma, she'll be your dad's angel on his shoulder from now on to repay him for stepping in last night." I looked over to Skylar sitting on a chair beside her mom's bed.

"You know me too well, child." Her mom smiled, patting Skylar's cheek. "Hello, Alexandra. I'm Jenny, and I owe my life to your father." I glanced back at Dad who was now blushing. "Your Dad has told me so much about you; I feel I know you already."

"The same goes with me," Dad said, looking at Skylar. "I've heard all about you."

"I'm sure she's had wonderful things to say about me." Skylar rolled her eyes, but smiled at the same time.

"That's right, girl. How you never listen, how you wear that junk on your face, and how you're doing the whole football team because of your reputation." She grinned. I choked, and I was sure Dad did as well, only he hid it behind a cough.

"You forgot the baseball team as well, Momma; how could you?" Sky glared. My Dad and I started laughing. I had just witnessed the very wonderful, sweet, but strange relationship Skylar and her mom had.

"So I see you two have already met," Dad said.

"Yes, last night," Skylar said.

"We're going for coffee later," I added.

"Oh, Mick. I do hope your daughter might be able to rub off some niceness onto my brat of a teenager."

"I don't know about that; yours seems normal enough. It may help my bookworm of a daughter to get out more, instead of taking care of the house and her father."

Skylar scoffed and said, "Now, now, 'rents. Where would the two of you be if we weren't around?"

"Rich." Mrs James smiled.

"Sane," my dad offered. I hit him in the arm. "Ow. See? Look at that abuse."

"Children these days." Mrs James shook her head. Both our parents laughed at their own joke. Skylar and I raised our eyebrows at each other.

We all looked to the door as a nurse walked in. "Sorry girls, but it's time for them to rest."

I looked down at Dad; he seemed tired. I wanted to stay longer, but I knew he needed his rest.

Skylar must have read the same from her mum, because she said, "Momma, you look buggered. You need to rest so you can get home to cook me tea, woman."

Mrs James laughed and then said, "A rest would be good, baby girl."

I looked down at Dad; he smiled up at me, nodded, and said, "It's okay, sweetheart. I'm fine now, and I'll be out in no time." I gave him a hug and a kiss on the cheek.

"I'll be back later," I whispered.

He shook his head. "Don't worry about it; you look beat. Go home, get some rest, and come and see me tomorrow after school. I'm sure the doctors will be letting me out then anyway."

"We'll see. I love you, Dad."

"You too, sweetheart, and I am sorry to scare you."

I nodded, gave him one last squeeze, and walked to the door. I waved my goodbye at a teary Mrs. James; she waved back over Skylar's shoulder.

TWENTY-FIVE

SKYLAR

Jessie met us down the street at a small coffee book house. One that I'd never been to before, but Alex had, and she was driving, so I let her choose the place. It wasn't too bad. It was a nice, warming, pleasant atmosphere with quiet music playing in the background.

I introduced Jessie—who was already waiting out the front —to Alex, and then went on to fill her in after Jessie yelled at me for not calling her last night to tell her what had happened with our parents.

Jessie gasped. "Holy heck."

Alex giggled at Jessie's usage of words. "That does sum it up nicely," she said.

I then went on about my night with Kane before I had that frightening phone call. When I mentioned Donna, Jessie breathed, "Dog." And I couldn't agree more.

It was when I got to the part about what had occurred that morning that both Jessie and Alex stared at me with wide eyes and mouths open.

"Oh, my freaking God," Jessie said, and sat back in her chair.

"Wow," Alex sighed.

"I know. But no matter how many times I tell him that it just isn't going to happen between us. He gets all…"

"Alpha hot male," Jessie offered.

"Yes. It drives me crazy. I just need him to get it through his head that it ain't gonna happen."

"Why can't it?" Alex asked.

"Yeah! Girl, you're crazy turning down someone that fine."

I shook my head. I should have realised that they wouldn't understand. "It won't work…and if I did happen to let something happen between us, it'll kill me in the end. *When* things do go bad, 'cause they will. His mother hates me; I don't know about his dad, but I know his mother would never approve of me in his life. I'd never want to cause trouble in his family life, and…we're just too different." I took a sip of my coffee, and watched Alex and Jessie share a glance. I had to smile; it was like Alex had been around us all our lives. She just fit right in.

Alex cleared her throat. "Sky, I know we don't know each other well, but I can already tell that when you talk about Kane, your whole face lights up. Wouldn't that type of happiness be worth any sort of trouble?"

Would it? I didn't know. It scared me. All of it.

"You know she's right, hooker," Jessie said as she placed her hand over mine on the table. "Though, I *do* know you, and you'll fight this in every way." She leaned back and grinned. "But I think you've met your match with Kane, and I think he's right. He will wear you down."

"No, he won't." I glared at them both.

"See? Stubborn. Alex, get used to it; she's like this all the time."

I rolled my eyes. "Whatever. Let's move on to your problem, Alex, and then we'll get to you, Jessie. Don't think I've forgotten about Mitch."

Jessie sighed. "Mine's straight forward, so I'll go first, because from the look in your eyes, Alex, your troubles seem more in depth." Jessie reached out and patted Alex's hand, and then continued, "Mitch went his own Alpha male way on me, and it was hot, so hot that now we're dating. I've started to notice the way he's been watching me—"

"Finally," I groaned.

"What? You knew? How long and why haven't you said anything?" she screeched.

"Probably because I know you, Jessie, and I know that you wouldn't have been interested if I had said anything back at the start of the year when I guessed it."

"Well, that's true. Okay, anyway. I'd told Mitch the other day that I was going out on a date...not that I was, but I wanted to see what he'd do." She grinned. "He said, 'Bullshit, you ain't going anywhere with anyone but me. From now frigging on, you and me are together.' That was when he kissed me, and I melted into a puddle of goo."

"That is so sweet," Alex said.

"Like I said, about time." I smiled. "Now that's been settled; Alex you're up." I nudged her foot with mine under the table.

"Oh, um. Mine isn't as exciting as any of yours."

"Girl, that doesn't matter, but we can see something's beating you up inside, and it's best to get it out," Jessie said.

"Okay. Well, I usually would tell my friend Sarah about this...but it kind of involves her. Sort of. You see there's this guy at my school—"

"The one who was at the hospital last night?" I asked, and when she nodded, I informed Jessie, "He was one huge, hot piece of meat, and I mean that with a capital H. He also looked like a badass; is he?" I asked.

"Yes. That's also the problem...I mean, not that I have anything against it," she looked down to the table and mumbled, "and really, it wasn't like anything would have happened between us."

"Alex," I said, and when she looked up, I added, "why don't you start from the beginning?"

She nodded. "My friend Sarah came to school one Monday

and informed me that she had kissed Tristan—the one you saw last night— and at first I felt sick because she knew that I didn't like him and his crew; they are mean and...bullies. But she also said that he was different and that she really liked him. Of course, I supported her, though I still worried. But then one afternoon, my Maths teacher asked me to be Tristan's tutor. I had no other option but to agree. He warned me to never say anything to anyone. So I didn't. But then we...I guess I could say we grew close, became friends. Secret friends, of course; he could never tell his friend about me—the nerdy loser from school. I could also never tell Sarah; she was falling for him more and more. I have never felt so guilty, but also...jealous. Of course, the more time I spent with Tristan, the more I liked him, so the more my feelings grew. One night, he turned up at my house; he'd been in a fight. I helped fix him up, and he kissed me in return. But that's all it ever was, a thank you kiss. Of course, my feelings didn't think that way." She took a sip of her latte and looked at us with tears shining in her eyes. I wanted to reach out and hug her, but she continued.

"Last night, he helped me in more ways than one. As soon as I'd received that awful phone call, my brain shut down. He barked out orders and got me to the hospital; he took care of me. He got me home and stayed...with me, in my bed. But..." She bit her bottom lip. "This morning, when he thought I was asleep, he woke up and swore, then said, 'What was I thinking?' and I didn't understand it at first. Then I pretended to wake up; it was then he informed me that nothing had changed between us, that he could never date someone like me. He doesn't need or want my help any longer with Maths."

"What a frigging ass," Jessie hissed.

I nodded and asked, "What did you say to him?"

"I told him that I understood that someone like him could never have feelings for someone like me, and that I knew nothing would have ever come of us because of those facts. I also told him that he was an ass for saying all that to me after the night I'd just had."

"Good for you," I said.

"I then went on to tell him I was going for a shower and that I expected him gone when I was out...and then, before...before I broke, I whispered his own words to him. I said, 'you're right, Tristan. What the hell were you thinking?'"

"Was he there when you came out?" Jessie asked.

"No," Alex whispered.

"Jesus, Alex. No wonder you looked so shattered when I saw you this morning. But, honey, he isn't worth it. Still, I don't get it. I saw him with you last night—the way he was looking at you...it doesn't make sense." I shook my head.

"If you ask me, I think he's more concerned about his street crew than anything, and that makes him a big jerk." Jessie said. "Forget him, Alex. I know it's going to be hard, but move on."

"I still think he'll come begging," I added.

"That's nice of you to say, Skylar. Very doubtful, but nice. So do you...do you think I should tell Sarah about everything?"

Jessie and I shared a look. I knew we were both thinking of my idiot-ex. So that was why I said, "Yeah, I think it needs to be done."

She nodded, took out her phone, and texted someone. Her phone pinged back straight away.

We watched Alex push her glasses back up her nose and then say, "She's meeting me at my house in an hour. Wish me luck."

"If she's any true friend, you won't need it," I said.

TWENTY-SIX

ALEXANDRA

Two weeks passed by, and in that time, everything had settled down in my life. Skylar and Jessie had been right. Sarah understood why I had kept everything from her; she was hurt, but she forgave me. She also agreed with Skylar, that Tristan would come crawling back because she saw the way he was with me that night at Joe's. The possessiveness and intense gaze while he watched me make out with that...idiot...clued her in.

Like I had said, I doubted it, and I was right. I no longer saw him outside of school, and even in school, he ignored me in every way. I no longer existed to him and his crew.

It hurt, not because he didn't reciprocate my feeling, but because I'd lost a friendship. Still, I could understand why he had done it this way, and I think he'd done it for my benefit, even though he was an ass about it. But if he hadn't cut me loose, I would have hungered for something more than friendship, worse than I already did, and it would have ruined everything. There was also the fact that he would have been embarrassed if anyone had seen us together...the nerd and the badass. They just didn't mix.

So I had to move on.

Even though there wasn't a day that went by when I didn't

think of him, or of the kiss we shared, or the way he'd held me all night.

Until his truthful, but hurtful words would crash through my mind and cut me deeply once again.

My dad had stayed in the hospital for three more days, and once he came home, things changed even more than what they had before he'd been hurt. He quit his job and was going to become an accountant with a firm that had a firm belief that family came first.

Last Saturday, he went on his first date since my mother had passed away...with Mrs Jones, Skylar's mum.

After he left, I rang Skylar, and we had a great laugh at how nervous they were. Secretly though, we were both thrilled by it.

"Alex, are you with me?" Sarah asked as a chip hit my chin.

"Sorry, what?"

Aaron, who was now a regular at the table because Sarah and he were dating, snorted and then laughed. "Off with the fairies again, Alex?"

At first, both Corbet and I worried he'd be his usual annoying self and tease us in every way when he started to join us for lunch. Only he didn't. It had a lot to do with Sarah, but lately, in the last couple of days, he actually seemed as though he liked hanging with us. He was nice, and often joined in our conversations.

I asked Sarah one time what Tristan thought of Aaron being around us all the time. She replied with a sad smile and said that Tristan didn't seem to care; he was happy for Aaron.

Aaron's friends still gave him hell for the change in his life. Still, Aaron didn't care; he'd give just as much as he received, and in the end, to my and Corbet's shock, they sometimes joined us as well.

Never Tristan, though.

I smiled at Aaron and said, "Yes, they're a better company than you guys."

Sarah giggled as Aaron kissed her neck.

"Hey, I'm not that bad," Corbet said, as he sat down at our table in the cafeteria.

"Thank goodness you're here. These two have been at each other the whole time; at least now, I'll have someone to talk to."

Corbet looked across the table to Sarah, and she longingly gazed at Aaron as he whispered something to her.

"I see what you mean," Corbet said and rolled his eyes.

"Hey, Corbet, when did you get here?" Aaron asked. Both Corbet and I laughed. "Listen, you wanna try that new video game this weekend?"

"Sure, at your place or mine?"

"Even better—mine," Sarah said. "My parents are going away for the week..." Sarah trailed off and looked behind me.

I felt who it was even before Aaron spoke, "Hey, man. What you doing gracin' us with you presence?" Aaron grinned.

"I just want to talk to Alex," Tristan barked.

Sarah looked at me. She studied me before she said, "Sorry, she doesn't want to talk to you."

Sighing in defeat, I closed my eyes. Sarah was right; I did not want to talk to him.

Two weeks.

He had a lot of chances before, but it had been two miserable weeks, and no matter what he had to say, I did not want to hear it.

"Man, maybe it's best if ya just go," Aaron said quietly.

"No." I knew from Tristan's tone that he was now glaring. I felt his heat move from my back to my side. "Alexandra?"

I opened my eyes to see him crouched beside my chair. His eyes pleaded, but once they saw my own eyes fill with tears, the look upon his face was regretful.

Shaking my head, I stood and turned to the others. "I—I'm going to go. I'll see you later."

"Okay." Sarah smiled sadly at me. Aaron sent me a chin lift, and even his eyes showed pity. Corbet grabbed my hand and gave it a reassuring squeeze, which I returned.

Pushing my chair back, I moved away as Tristan stood and grabbed wrist. "Alexandra, please, just hear me out."

The cafeteria went silent. I could see all the students looking our way. They were probably in hope for some sort of scene to entertain them in any way. Only I would not allow it to be me.

I spun back to Tristan, got close enough to stand on my tippy toes, and glare into his eyes. "Leave me alone," I hissed.

He let go of my wrist. Let go of me. I made it five steps away, I counted them, when he called out, "What I said that morning—it wasn't how it sounded."

I froze.

Now, I wanted to hear what he had to say, but not in front of everyone. I was about to turn and tell him that when he continued.

In front of everyone.

"I said I didn't know what I was thinking because I knew…I knew I couldn't be around you without…without feeling the way I did about you."

People gasped. Some laughed.

Turning, I pleaded with my eyes and a shake of my head for him to stay silent. He had to know what I was thinking as I surveyed the many students listening in. I couldn't let…whatever this was…happen in front of so many people.

"Tristan," I whispered, "don't—"

"I don't give a shit about what they think." He gestured to the room in general. He started walking towards me, only to stop a few steps away. "I'm sorry I hurt you, and the time I chose to do it. I'm sorry I haven't cleared this up before now. Jesus, I'm sorry for being a chicken shit and caring about what people would say, what your father would say if you brought someone like me home as…as your boyfriend."

My hand flew to my mouth. I heard Sarah sob behind Tristan. Students started talking in low voices, but all I could do was stare at Tristan as his eyes warmed and he smiled down at me.

Tears now ran freely down my cheeks as I continued to stare with wide eyes.

He was telling the room, telling everyone here that he wanted to be with me.

But he had hurt me.

Just because he was willing to do this in front of so many, did that give him a right to expect me to forgive him for the way he'd treated me?

He took another step towards me, only that time, I backed up a step, shaking my head. I moved my hand away from my mouth and asked, "Why are you doing this?"

"Because I hate what I am without you. I used to look forward to those days we had together when you tutored me in Maths. I looked forward to spending time with you. To the text messages. Crap, I sound like a tool, but I miss you. I miss not seeing you smile, not hearing your voice. I can only hope you'll forgive me."

"Under the thumb," someone yelled.

"Rack off, dickhead," Tristan growled. The room fell silent once again.

He took a step forward and I didn't move. He reached out and ran the back of his hand down the side of my cheek, gently wiping away my tears.

As soon as he knew I wasn't going to protest, he pulled me into his arms, wrapping me tightly in his embrace. He kissed my neck and whispered into my ear, "I will regret the words I said to you for the rest of my life. I didn't mean any of it. You are more my type than anyone else in this room, and I will spend the rest of our time together making it up to you…"

My breath hitched; his words knocked the breath out of me. I gripped his tee and his waist. I wasn't sure whether it was to pull him closer, or if it was for the support to help me stand on my two weak legs.

"I know we still have a long way to go before I even start to make it up to you, but every second will be worth it because *you* are worth it."

I bit my bottom lip as he stood straight to study my face.

Clearing my throat, I said, "Y—you didn't need to do…say this…in front of everyone."

He chuckled. "I did. You can't tell me that if I turned up at your place that you'd answer the door. Or you would have sent me away. I also wanted to do this in front of our peers to show to you and to myself, that I didn't care what anyone thinks. Besides, if they do say shit, I'll just beat the hell outta them." He grinned and then sobered. "I have to be honest. It scared the hell out of me to do this. But once I saw you sitting there without a smile on your beautiful face, I knew I had to do it. I had to have you smile again. I had to take away your pain. The pain that I caused. I knew I had to go to great lengths…do *you* know why, Alexandra?"

My heart beat wildly as I shook my head, and then whispered, "No."

He bent lower so our noses touched, and I watched his eyes crinkle as he smiled. "Because I love you." And then he kissed me.

In front of everyone.

Cheers started, along with whistles and shouting. But I ignored it all and was swept away with the moment.

He was right. We had a long way to go before things were great between us, but I knew that I would enjoy working it out along the way.

SKYLAR

EPILOGUE

I had the chance to hide from Kane for two weeks because I hadn't gone to school. My teachers understood that I wanted to be at home with Momma. It wasn't that he didn't try to come around. He did, multiple times, and once Momma knew I wasn't going to answer the door or speak with him, she, in her polite way, told him to give me time, that I had a screw loose.

Even when I told her after the first time he came, it just wouldn't work between the two of us because we were from different worlds. She scoffed and told me to get my head out of my butt.

It was good to see her back to normal. I have never been worried like that before in my whole life, and I never wanted to be again.

The one great thing that did come from the accident was Alex. She's like the sister I'd never had. Every day we talked over the phone. What was also great was that Momma had her first date in...well, a long time, with Alex's dad, and I couldn't have chosen a more perfect guy for her.

It was great to see her fuss, and be shy and embarrassed over her first date. It gave me a lot of ammunition to tease her with.

But what was more than great, better than anything so far, was to see my momma happy.

"Skylar, will you get that damn phone?" Momma yelled from the living area.

Honestly, I hadn't even heard it. I got up from my bed and took the seven steps out into the kitchen to grab the phone on the wall.

"Hello?"

"Hi, is this Skylar?" A deep male voice asked.

"Yeeeah?"

"Oh, good. Skylar, this is Mr Stanley, Dommy's father."

My heart jumped into my throat, and I gripped the phone harder.

"Is everything all right? Is Dommy okay? Kane?"

He chuckled. "Yes, sorry to scare you after everything you have been through. I was only calling...you see, I have to be at a meeting soon, and Rosa has a doctor's appointment, and Kane is at school. He mentioned you hadn't been attending, so I was hoping you would be able to mind Dommy for me?"

I deflated my tense shoulders and said, "Oh, um...I think I can make it. Let me just check with my momma."

"Of course."

I covered the mouth piece and turned to Momma, who was sitting on the couch watching *Dr Phil*. "Momma—"

"Go, get."

"But you don't even know where. For all you know, it could be some drug dealer on the phone asking if I'd sell crack to school kids."

"And I'd be fine with that if it got you out of this house. You're driving me crazy."

I sighed and put the phone back up to my ear. "Mr Stanley, I would love to come and play with Dommy."

"Great. Do I need to send a car for you?"

And there we have yet another reason why Kane and I were worlds apart.

"No thanks. The bus should be past here soon. I'll just catch that. Only if that's okay, I mean, can you wait until I get there for your meeting?"

"Yes, I can wait. See you when you get here, Skylar."

He hung up and left me thinking he was nicer than what I had first thought. Maybe it was just Kane's mother who hated me and thought I was a nobody.

Standing out the front of Kane's house for the first time since that night sent chills down my spine. I looked up to the shining sun and was thankful once again that everything was good.

Walking up the drive, I suddenly felt nervous. I could only hope that Mr Stanley would be home before Kane had the chance to get home from school. I looked at my watch. Three hours should be enough for a meeting, right?

I knocked on the front door, and it opened quickly to a smiling Mr Stanley.

"Skylar, thank you very much for coming." He gestured for me to enter, so I stepped in.

"Not a problem. I think Momma was actually starting to get sick of me at home anyway. She'll probably have me back at school next week."

He laughed. "I've got to head out now. I think Dommy's in the library."

"Okay, thanks." I moved off towards the library.

"Skylar?"

I turned. "Yes?"

"Mrs Stanley and I are no longer...together. So I hope to see you here more often. I know Dommy has missed you."

Oh. Wow. That was nice of him. Strange, but nice.

"Um, I guess...I...Dommy could come to my house anytime to see me. Anytime you need her watched, I'd be more than happy to see her."

He smiled and nodded. I turned back around and walked off once again. I heard the front door open and close before I reached for the door handle to the library.

Opening it and stepping through, I couldn't see Dommy anywhere. Maybe she was playing hide-and-seek. So I called to the room, "Come out wherever you are." Smiling to myself, I started looking behind chairs.

When I was down on my hands and knees looking under the large table and chairs where Kane and I studied, I heard the library door open.

The little sneak was playing me.

I jumped up, ready to run after her, only to stop, my hand flying to my chest as my heart sped when I came face-to-face with Kane.

"W—what are you doing here? Where's Dommy?"

He smiled down at me. "Dommy's out with Dad for the afternoon."

I scowl at him and placed my hands on my hips. "What do you mean she's out with your dad? I'm supposed to be minding her."

"Sky, don't be too mad. This was the only way I was going to get to see you." He took a step closer. I backed up one.

"Your dad was in on this?"

His smile widened. "It was his idea. He was sick of seeing me mope around."

"Why? Why would he do this?"

I didn't understand.

"He knows *who* would make me happy, so he's gone about to...hopefully, fix this—us."

"Us?" I shook my head. "There is no us."

He stepped closer again. "I want there to be," he uttered.

Looking at the floor, I whispered back, "No. You don't. You can't."

"I do and I can. Donna and I are never getting back together; she isn't the one that plays on my mind constantly. She isn't the one for me. Even my dad knew this."

"Don't you see the trouble you'll get if you rock up to school...with me at your side?"

"Is that the only reason holding you back? Because I don't give a shit what everyone thinks, and I thought you were the same." He reached for me and placed his hands on my waist, pulling me closer so our feet touch. "I only want to be with you."

My heart felt like it was thumping so hard in my chest it would burst out. Did I want this? Hell yeah. But I was scared that this—us, being together, would come and bite us both on the ass and cause us nothing but trouble.

So was I willing to take the risk? For us to come together and give...a relationship with Kane a go?

Yes!

I looked up into his eyes, and whatever he saw in my own eyes had him smiling so wide I thought his face would crack, and then he was kissing me.

No matter what anyone would say. No matter what anyone would think. This was worth it. He was worth it. Because Kane could certainly kiss.

ACKNOWLEDGMENTS

To *my family and friends* for all the support and encouragement throughout this process.

To *Becky* at *Hot Tree Editing*: I know I say this all the time, but you are awesome and without you and *Kayla the Bibliophile* I would have given up.

To *my street team*: I love all of you girls and guy each in your own way.

Lindsey, you are a godsend. I am so glad to have met you!

To *all the readers, bloggers and fellow authors* who have helped me along the way.

I have made new friends and I am grateful for each and every one of you.

ALSO BY LILA ROSE

Hawks MC: Ballarat Charter

Holding Out (FREE): Zara and Talon

Climbing Out: Griz and Deanna

Finding Out (novella): Killer and Ivy

Black Out: Blue and Clarinda

No Way Out: Stoke and Malinda

Coming Out (novella): Mattie and Julian

Hawks MC: Caroline Springs Charter

The Secret's Out: Pick, Billy, and Josie

Hiding Out: Dodge and Willow

Down and Out: Dive and Mena

Living Without: Vicious and Nary

Walkout (novella): Dallas and Melissa

Hear Me Out: Beast and Knife

Breakout (novella): Handle and Della

Fallout: Fang and Poppy

Standalones related to the Hawks MC

Out of the Blue (Lan, Easton, and Parker's story)

Trinity Love Series

Left to Chance

Love of Liberty (novella)

Young Adult

Senseless Attraction

Romantic Comedies

Making Changes

Making Sense

Fumbled Love

Paranormal

Death (with Justine Littleton)

In the Dark